I GOT NOTHING BUT LOVE FOR MY HITTA 2

JAHQUEL J.

TEXT UCP TO 22828 TO SUBSCRIBE TO OUR MAILING LIST

If you would like to join our team, submit the first 3-4 chapters of your completed manuscript to

Submissions@UrbanChapterspublications.com

1

KASH

ALL I COULD HEAR WAS the constant beeping sound around me. My throat felt like I had cotton in it, and my body felt like it was run over by a bus. Each time I tried to move, it was too painful, so I stayed still. My eyes felt like I had crust in them, and my chest was heavy. What the fuck was going on? I took a deep breath and decided to pry my eyes open, one lid at a time. When I finally got them open, I looked around the room. The lights were turned off, but the sun came through the blinds. I saw a wheelchair, machines, and a chair that held a blanket in it. The blanket was crumpled up as if someone was sitting there. I cleared my throat, but it was too painful. I closed my eyes back again just to rest them for a minute. I barely moved, but the shit was so painful that I had to take a break.

I was about to doze off when I heard someone mumbling to themselves. I opened my left eye quick and took a glimpse. The person had their back turned, so I couldn't see it who it was.

"Yo," I whispered. My voice was low, but I was sure they heard me. They stopped mumbling and turned around and faced me. When they turned around, my eyes got all misty. "Princess," I croaked.

She rushed over to my side and looked at me. I could tell she had gotten thicker from the baby. *Damn, how long I been out?* All I remembered was being shot and seeing white lights.

"Kash, baby, you're awake... Nurse!" she yelled and walked to the doorway. The nurse came walking through the doorway, and Chyna walked back over to the bed. "He's awake! Y'all said he wouldn't wake up, and look now," she bragged and kissed me on the forehead. The nurse walked in and looked at me. I was staring back at her, and she gasped.

"You're right. Let me go get the doctor right away," she said and shuffled out the door.

Chyna caressed my face as she looked at me. "Babe, I swear I fought until they listened. They tried to take you off last month, and I fought with them." She choked on the tears.

"Ma, I—"

"Stop talking with that tube in your mouth. Once the doctor comes, then you'll be able to speak with me," she cut me off.

I looked into her beautiful face and could tell my situation had been causing her so much stress. I wanted to know how my son was doing and just how long I'd been out. Shit was still blurry to me, but I wanted to get out of here and handle shit. Who was running BMS? There was a lot of shit that I had to find out.

"Mr. Lozada, you've really proven that you want to be here on this green Earth." The doctor walked into the room. She rinsed her hands then walked over to the bed with the gloves. She looked over the vital signs that the nurse had taken and nodded her head.

"Do you think I should take his tube out?" she asked the residents that followed behind her closely. I looked at Chyna, and she already knew what I was thinking. They weren't about to touch me with their eager asses.

One with glasses on and a notepad stepped up. "Yes. I can imagine that it's causing so much discomfort. His pulse indicates that his breathing is fine, and he looks very alert to me," she looked at me and explained.

"Thank you, Dr. Yuzi," she said and stepped closer to me. The residents all moved closer to see her remove the tube. "Alright, Mr. Lozada. This will be uncomfortable for a bit," she warned and started to take the tube apart, then slid it out my throat. Fuck discomfort—that shit hurt like hell. If my arms weren't so weak, I would put her head through the wall.

She positioned my bed up, and I started coughing up in the pink basin she provided. That shit felt like I had a blunt that was lit in my throat. I continued to cough and gag until the feeling to do so ceased.

"We'll keep you sitting up so you can spit any excess fluids out. You still can't eat any foods for about four days, so we'll continue to feed you with the tube in your stomach. After a few days, if you're doing fine, I'll consider giving you some real food."

"What about pissing? I want to take a piss," my scratchy voice asked.

She laughed and held up a bag filled with piss that was beside me. "You can just urinate. You have a catheter in. Since you haven't walked, I want to give you a few days before we get you on your feet. I don't want to push you too fast." She patted my hand.

"How long I've been here?"

"A month and a half." Chyna whimpered and held my hand. She wiped the tear from her eyes and looked at me. "Kairo, I really thought I lost you." She cried.

My hands felt like cement bricks were holding them down, but I held them up so she could give me a hug. She gently came into my arms and hugged me.

"I'm not going nowhere," I promised her.

She cried, and I held her the best I could. I knew I shouldn't have been looking, but my eyes wandered on that round ass. Chyna had always had an ass, but that shit got bigger, and I couldn't act like I didn't see it.

"How's my son?"

She pulled back and looked at me. I tried to move over so she could sit, but she pulled the chair closer to my side.

"He's fine; I want him to meet his daddy. I haven't been much of a mother, Kairo," she admitted.

"Quit calling me that," I told her.

"I need to start because your son's name is Kash, and I don't want y'all to be confused." She laughed.

"His name gon' be Lil' Kash. I ain't changing my name," I joked with her.

She grabbed my hand and looked me in the face. "Babe, I really thought I lost you. I need to go call everybody and let them know. I've been so caught up on you waking up that I forgot."

I nodded my head, and she left the room to make the call. I needed to find some things out, and I knew Benji had to know. I laid back and waited for everybody to come and see me. I wanted to see my son. I laid my eyes on him once, and he was already a month old. They tried to take me down once, but there wasn't about to be a second time, and I put that on my life.

2

LEYANNA

"BENJI, for once, can you grab the phone?" I groaned as I turned over and closed my eyes again. He insisted on keeping the phone on his side but never wanted to answer the damn thing.

"Here." He tossed the phone and pulled the covers over his head. I sat up, looked at the time, and gasped. I pressed the button and answered the phone while rubbing my forehead.

"Hello?"

"Leyanna, Kash is up!" Chyna screamed through the phone. I could tell Benji heard her because he sat up in the bed.

"What? We're on our way!" I screamed, happy that he was awake. The doctors didn't have hope for him, but Chyna wouldn't allow them to pull the plug. She was there every day at least three times a day.

I had been wanting to have a talk about her leaving her baby so much, but Benji suggested I didn't. He told me that Chyna was going through a lot, and she had to do this. He explained how it was when their mother passed, and I understood. I helped out with the baby as much as I could, but with school and the store, I was doing the most. Some nights, I didn't get to bed until around three. Kash's parents had moved into his place with Chyna to help with their grandchild. They were the only shining light in this whole thing. They helped with Baby Kash and Chyna because she was mentally losing it. A few times, I had to go and take her home because she had been up there all day.

"Tell her I'm on my way," Benji grumbled and pulled the covers off his body. I looked at his chiseled frame and his dreads hanging wild. "I'm 'bout to go pray. Don't take all day, Ley," he warned me and walked out the room.

"Chy, I'm going to shower and get dressed. I'll see you soon," I promised her. We spoke for a few then we ended the call.

I got out the bed and went to the bathroom to shower and change. Benji got up and went to his rug to do his morning prayers. After showering and grabbing anything from the bin of clothes I had acquired at Benji's house, I was ready. Meanwhile, this man of mine was just grabbing a towel and heading to the bathroom.

"Really, Benji?"

He looked unbothered as he grabbed his shit and went into the bathroom. I shook my head and went into the kitchen to get me some coffee. We didn't have time to prepare a breakfast, so I popped some toast into the toaster and spread some organic jelly. Benji didn't trust regular jelly because he swore they used pork fat in it, so this man found a lady that actually made homemade organic grape jelly and paid $20 a jar. Don't get me wrong, it was really good, but not for some damn $20.

Twenty minutes later, Benji came downstairs and grabbed some toast and the keys.

"You ready?"

"I've been ready. Been waiting on you," I said as we walked out the door and got into the car.

Benji pulled out as he was munching on his piece of toast. It was then I realized that I forgot mine on the counter. Grabbing a lollipop out of the center console, I opened it and started sucking on it. I prayed now that Kash was up that this would allow her to focus on her. She had been letting school fall by the wayside, and it wasn't good at all.

"Babe, you got jelly on your lips," I said and leaned up and over to kiss him on the lips to remove it.

"Ley, I'll beat your ass if you put your lips on mine after sucking on that pork stick," he threatened, and I sat back down.

The red light changed to green, and we pulled into the parking lot of the hospital.

"You so extra." I laughed because he was serious and wasn't messing with me. We parked and headed into the hospital, hand in hand.

3

BENJI

THAT NIGGA KASH was fucked up and had to recover before thinking about getting in the streets. I had been following what was going on in his absence, but I kept a low profile. I didn't like niggas knowing what I had going on. The same niggas that doubted me and underestimated me were the same niggas lying in ditches. When Kash sent everyone to the cafeteria for some sushi, I knew they didn't have nor did he want, I pulled a chair up. Mookie argued that there was none yet took her ass anyway.

"What's good, nigga?" he said and held his hand out.

I dapped him and looked him in the eye. I knew Allah had a lot of faith and strength in me because I was staring my mother's murderer in his eyes. I left the shit alone and prayed about it for a long time. I almost felt like him getting shot was because I was praying about the situation too hard. When I looked at how broken and in pain Mookie was over him, I knew I made the right choice by not taking matters into my own hands. She loved the shit out that nigga, and each time I picked up my nephew, I saw Kash in him. How could I live with knowing I killed his father? What Kash did, he would have to live with for the rest of his life. That was punishment enough for me.

"How you holding up?" I looked at him.

He winced as he tried to position himself. "Nigga, this shit is so fucking painful. I just want to know if you had something to do with this?"

I laughed and stood up. I walked over to the window and looked at the sun shining brightly. "You think you would be asking that question if I did?"

He nodded and still held eye contact with me. "What about JoJo?"

"Nah, asked him the same thing."

"How you know?"

"I know my brother, and he wouldn't lie to me. He said he's not your friend, but he'll spare you because of his love for Mookie. Swore on my goddaughter and is even down with getting whoever," I explained.

He sighed a breath of relief and laid his head back. "How's BMS? I know you heard some things."

"A fuckin' mess. Shit been wild between BMS and GB. You need to have your niggas calm down and lay low... I know for a fact shit with your supplier ain't gon' be sweet." I could tell he was thinking about how he was gonna explain shit to his supplier.

"Shit, I forgot all about Chuba." He sighed. "Benji, I need you to do me a solid, and I know you don't owe me shit but I need this," he begged.

I crossed my arms and looked at him. "What?"

"I need you to handle BMS until further notice. I worked hard to make that shit what it is, and I'll be damned if it goes to hell."

"You already know I can't step into that. I lay low for a reason, you know that," I told him. As much as I wanted to help him out, I couldn't. I stayed low because of the line of work I did.

I made sure I handled shit and got ghost so I could live a regular life. 'No face, no case' was my motto, and I lived by that shit.

"I wanna meet with JoJo."

I laughed until I saw that he was dead serious. "JoJo ain't your biggest fan, and you already know that."

"Look, I don't give a fuck; I just need someone who is willing to be savage. I need a nigga that'll handle shit and sleep like a baby at night. Benj, I don't know you like that, but I know you pray for forgiveness at night for your sins while JoJo is on his second wind of sleep. If you won't do it, I know he'll do it, no problem."

He had a point, but JoJo wasn't about to help him out with BMS. I mean, I could ask him, but I knew he wouldn't do it. When I found Kash laying in that warehouse damn near dead, I had two choices. I could leave him there to die or help him out. I decided to help him out, and the whole time, I thought that JoJo had something to do with it. I pulled a gun out on my brother for Kash. I had to know that he wouldn't go against my word. I had to know he didn't just make my sister a single mother.

"Why the fuck you did it, JoJo?" I rammed him into the wall with a gun in his face. He looked at the gun and back at me with a grimace.

"Fuck you talking about, Benji!" he yelled and shoved me off him, looking at me with fire in his eyes.

"Why the fuck you get at Kash like that! I told you to calm that shit down and let me handle shit!" I barked and pushed him into the wall.

A genuinely confused expression crossed his face. "Nigga, I been here all day! Fuck you talking about? I ain't thinking about that nigga! So you put a gun in your brother's face over a nigga that killed your moms!" he yelled back.

"I just left that nigga at the hospital. Followed him to some

warehouse, and he was slumped. You telling me you didn't have shit to do with that?" I walked near him and looked into his eyes.

"I put that shit on Jolie's life. I ain't left the crib. Renee went to get some dinner because a nigga had a fucked up stomach!" he yelled and walked toward the balcony. He pushed over a picture of us on the floor. The glass shattered, and he punched the wall. "My own brother pulls a gun on me for some other nigga!" he yelled and his voice broke. His back was turned, but I could tell he was crying.

"I didn't mean that shit like that." Thinking back, I should have never pulled a gun on him. This wasn't some regular nigga that I was dealing with. This was my ace, right-hand, and brother. We'd been through the worst shit together, and he deserved more than how I approached him.

"Nah, fuck that shit. I would have never come to you like that. I respect anything you tell me, even if I don't believe in that shit. You told me to lay low, and that's what the fuck I did."

I walked over to him, and he snatched his hands away from me, but I still pulled him into a brotherly hug.

"I put that on Allah, I will always kick myself in the ass for this. You're my brother, my family. I should have never approached you like that," I told him and walked out the crib.

I looked up just in time to see Chyna and everyone walk back into the room. It had been a month since I spoke to JoJo. I knew he was good because he checked in on Chyna and the baby. What could I say to get us past this spot? A nigga waved a gun in his face, and that couldn't be forgiven easily.

"Baby, you alright?" Leyanna leaned on me. She looked up at me, and I nodded. I kissed her on the forehead and watched as Kash's mother fawned over him. I looked down at Leyanna and asked myself how did I get so lucky? She had been down for me since she met me and hadn't dimed me out.

"Mookie, I'm 'bout to head home. I got a flight tomorrow

morning," I said and hugged her. She hugged me back and smiled.

"You're leaving already? Okay, but I'll see you when you come back; be safe, Bee Bee," she told me.

"Bet; Kash, get better, nigga," I said and dapped him. "Nice seeing you again," I said to his parents.

I told Leyanna she could stay, but she grabbed my hand and left with me. I had to head to Arizona to get at this nigga who owed some kingpin money. I didn't get too involved in their shit. I just wanted to know when my money was coming, and how much the price was. I was set to leave in the morning. As always, I wanted to just pray and relax until the morning.

"You staying at my place?" I asked Leyanna, and she nodded her head.

I was all in with Ley; still, we hadn't moved in together. She wanted to take things slow, and I respected her wishes. I couldn't help but think of her being barefoot and pregnant when I looked at her. She wanted to do her thing and make her own bread, so I had to sit back and allow that.

"Benji," she called out. The car was quiet, and all that could be heard were the windshield wipers. All the sun had gone away, and the rain was out heavy now.

"What's up?"

"I want you to be careful when you're handling business—"

"Wiz, I told—"

She waved her hand up and cut me off. "I don't want to hear any of what you're about to say. The fact remains that you're doing a dangerous job. Things could go wrong, although I pray hard that it never does. I just want you to always think of Chyna and your nephew when deciding on these jobs, babe."

"Nah."

"Nah?" she questioned.

"I don't think of them," I replied.

"Benji, that's who you shou—"

It was my turn to cut her statement short. "Chyna and Baby Kash is always on my mind when I make decisions, but I have to realize that Mookie is an adult with her own family now. She'll always be my baby girl, but she's a mother and fiancée now. I keep you and our future in the back of my head. I want to always make it back home so we can have a future."

I could feel her staring at me, and I knew her ass was about to get emotional. "I just want you to be careful. I worry about you and how long you're going to do this."

"This is all I know, Leyanna. Fuck you want me to do? You met me doing this shit!" I barked.

She jumped and remained quiet. She looked out the window and didn't say anything. When we pulled up, she opened the door and got out. Pulling her purse on her arm, she looked at me. "I think I should stay home for the night."

"Ley, come on," I called behind her, and she kept walking. Once I made sure she got in the crib, I walked into mine.

Mookie had been staying at Kash's house with his parents. I wanted her home, but I knew that wouldn't happen. She wanted to be close to Kash, and I had to respect that. I couldn't help but feel like I was losing Mookie.

"I was calling your phone, nigga," JoJo said when I walked into the kitchen. He was sitting at the table with a bowl of cereal.

I was shocked as shit to see him over my crib. We hadn't spoken since I pulled the gun on him, and I didn't think we would have a conversation for a while. JoJo knew how to hold a grudge if someone stole his piece of sandwich.

"Didn't think you would show up here. I was at the hospital; Kash woke up." I sat down on the couch and leaned my head back.

"Renee told me I should come over here and speak to you. I

told her 'fuck that nigga,' but you see I'm here." He chuckled and sat down beside me.

I laughed and kicked my feet up on the coffee table. "You already know how—"

"Water under the bridge; it was more for Mookie than it was for that nigga Kash. I get it," he cut me off and explained as he slurped his cereal.

"You see how bad she was stressing this past month and a half. I gotta sacrifice my feelings for her happiness."

"You think she would still be happy if she knew he killed y'all moms?" JoJo asked a valid question.

Mookie wouldn't be happy if she knew about Kash's involvement in our mother's death. She would probably be done with him and demand that I kill him. However, she didn't need to know any of that, and this was a secret I was taking to my grave. Mookie was so happy with this nigga, and it didn't help that his parents thought of her as their own, something she wanted for a while. His mother was a sweet woman that cared about Mookie and my nephew, along with her son.

"I doubt it. That's why we're going to keep this shit to ourselves," I warned him, and he nodded his head.

"I always keep my mouth shut, but I'm telling you that it's going to come out sooner than later. Skeletons never stay in the closet long, Benji."

"Yeah, ight... Why you over here?"

"Renee thinks she may be pregnant," JoJo revealed.

Last I remembered, JoJo wasn't ready to be a father when Jolie was about to be born. Yeah, he changed his ways and was a father to her now, but the fact remained that he complained all through Lilly's pregnancy. Financially, he was always there, but mentally and physically was another thing. Lilly called my jack a few times a night looking for this nigga.

"You want it?"

"Hell nah. I'm not ready to be that whole family man right now. I'm chilling and like Renee living with me along with Jolie, but bringing a new baby into that shit is wild." He sighed.

"She ain't on no birth control or some shit?"

"Nigga, I been checking for that shit since she moved in, and I haven't found it."

"You ain't ask her ass?"

He laughed and nodded his head. "Nah, but now she talking about babies and shit. We supposed to take a test tonight when I get home."

"Damn. Well, congrats!"

"I ain't ready for this shit right now," he complained and set his bowl down.

I got up from the couch, went into the fridge, and tossed him a beer. He popped the top off and took a slug before sitting it down. "You need to stop fucking her raw. You saying you don't want kids is one thing, but preventing them is another thing too, bruh."

He shook his head and finished his beer. "Where Ley?"

"Next door with an attitude." I smirked.

"Fuck you did to her now?"

"She chatting about me giving up the lifestyle I live. Talking about I can't do this shit forever... Who the fuck said I could?"

"She knows this is how you make your money besides the sneaker shop, right?"

"She thinks her little boutique gonna provide our lifestyle. I chilled on taking jobs, but I ain't about to stop cold turkey."

"So you're considering stopping?"

"Nah, but if we get to the point that she has my seed and becomes my wife, I would."

"Y'all ain't have no scare yet?"

"Nah, she made it clear she don't want kids right now."

JoJo jumped up and slapped his hands together. "Why can't I find a chick like that?"

"Nigga, you got a good woman, and you'll take care of the seed if she is," I told him and sat back on the couch.

JoJo stayed around for a little while before he dipped home to face Renee and the pregnancy test. I called Leyanna to come over to my crib, and she didn't answer. Since she had a little attitude, I figured I'd leave her alone and catch her when I got back from Arizona.

4

SOLACE

LILLY WAS GETTING on a nigga's nerves as she complained about shit. I tried my best to ignore and continued to lay in the bed. Damn, all a nigga wanted was some head and quiet around this bitch. Nah, she had to be all loud about me coming home late. Shit was crazy in the street, and if she thought I was about to sit and watch Lifetime with her ass, she had another thing coming. Shit had been crazy since she said she wanted to be done with our relationship. I told her ass she could dip and be gone. I didn't have an issue with skipping to the next broad. Her baby daddy was expecting a baby with his girl and had told her. Ever since he said that shit, she had been wanting to make shit work with us, except that all she did was argue and start shit for no reason.

"Go on with all that loud bullshit, Lilly." I waved her off.

I sighed when I heard her come out the bathroom, still going on. "I don't have to deal with this shit. I got my own and damn sure don't need to be arguing with a nothing ass!" she yelled and waved her hands.

I laughed and got off the bed. "You came back to make it work with this nigga tho'," I taunted.

"I'm a respected doctor in this town, and I don't need to be linked with a known drug dealer. Solace, we're done, and don't bother to call me when you're done being a dick!" she screamed and tossed the pack of condoms at me.

"How you know that's not from us?"

She looked at me and rolled her eyes. "You know we don't fuck with condoms. We've been trying for a baby, or did you forget? I'm kind of glad that I didn't get pregnant. I knew things would never work the second round. That's why I haven't brought Jolie or mom back in the house." She grabbed a bag and placed some clothes in it. She got frustrated and just closed the bag.

"Let me know when you're gone." I laid back on the bed and found a blunt on the side table. I lit the blunt and took small pulls as she walked in and out the room. I could tell my nonchalant behavior was pissing her off.

I had a million things to worry about, and Lilly with her insecure ass wasn't one of them. Her baby father might have played into that shit, but that wasn't me. GB had been taking losses left and right. BMS was on a warpath after I hit up Kash in that warehouse. I was happy I caught him right in time. Those out of town niggas had nothing to do with it, but I bodied their asses too and took the money; niggas were stupid anyway. I hadn't heard much from the streets about Kash. A nigga didn't know if he was dead or alive since it hadn't been a funeral. One of my young niggas said that his little shawty had been going up to the hospital almost every day. I assumed he was in a coma, which was just as good as dead. Lil' mama was probably holding on to a dream anyway. I hit that nigga a few times, and if he lived, he could call himself Jesus, and I would too.

I heard the front door slam and walked to the hall front

window. I watched as she threw bags into the back of her Jaguar and pulled out the driveway. I knew she would be back, so I had no worries. Lilly couldn't get enough of this dick and would continue to bring her ass around. Even if we didn't get back together, I knew I would still be hitting that shit sometime soon, so a nigga wasn't worried about this whole charade she just put on. I went into the kitchen and found me some leftovers she made from the night before. I grabbed a plate and fixed me some before heading into the living room to watch *Shottas*. I figured this shit would give me some inspiration on how I was going to wipe out BMS.

5

CHYNA

"CALM DOWN, babe. You don't have to take off running," I suggested, and he ignored me. He still walked fast with the physical therapist. I had just burped Lil' Kash and was watching his daddy work himself too hard.

It had been two weeks since he woke up, and things had been looking up. The tube was out of his stomach, and he was eating solid foods. His voice was still raspy from the tube, and the doctor told him that his throat would still remain sore. The nurses were bringing him too much tea to help with that. Each time I turned around, there was another one bringing him tea with a smirk. The way they called him Kash, because he refused them to call him Mr. Lozada, pissed me off. After week one, I knew he was wanting to be around the baby. Since he was in a private suite and didn't have any viruses, they agreed to allow me to bring him up here.

"Alright, Kash. I'll be back tomorrow at the same time. I hear the doctors want to release you by next week, so let's get you walking out of here." He clapped his hands.

Kash scooted back on the bed and grabbed the weights they

gave him to work his arms out. "Ight. I'll see you tomorrow," he said and started using the weights.

"Make sure he doesn't push himself too hard. He may feel great now, but things can go downhill quickly," the therapist warned.

"I'll make sure he's doing the minimum," I promised.

He smiled and walked out the room with his charts. I looked over at Kash as I placed our son back into his car seat. Each time I looked at my son, he reminded me so much of his father. Lil' Kash was his father's twin, and from the baby pictures, it was so true.

"I wish they stop trying to tell me about my own body." He winced as he lifted the weight with his left hand.

"Because they know what they're doing. Hardheaded patients make a mess of things."

"Princess, stop agreeing with they asses. I've been running sprints in here at night since two nights ago. Have I passed the fuck out?" He continued to lift the weights.

"Sprints? Kash, you need to really stop pushing yourself too hard. I know you want to get out of here, but what good are you if you pass out once we're home?"

I could tell what I said didn't mean a thing to him. I looked down at my baby and sighed at his father. I couldn't use the excuse anymore about Kash being in the hospital. He was back up, and it seemed he was back to himself. It was time for me to get back into school work and helping Leyanna with the shop. What other nineteen-year-old you knew that co-owned a shop? The month Kash had been in the hospital had been the worst time in my life. I was adjusting to being a mother when all I wanted to do was crawl up in the bed with him. I had to finish school and bring good grades. Benji would put his foot in my ass if I didn't. Looking at my son's face made me want to make him proud. He was far from expected, but I wouldn't allow the excuse I had a kid early mess up the plans I had for myself.

"Why you so quiet now, Princess?" He looked over at me.

"Just thinking about school and the shop," I replied.

"I know your ass hasn't been keeping up with that, and I feel like shit," he admitted.

"It's not your fault that someone shot and tried to kill you, baby. I'm going to handle school and running the shop, so don't worry about it. Your mother agreed to stay up here longer to help with the baby, so we'll be good," I reminded him.

I didn't want him to feel like it was his fault I hadn't been keeping up with my schooling. I had a meeting with the lady from my school. Online classes were only for students keeping up, so I knew she would tell me I had to return to school. I didn't mind; I needed to focus. Being home with a newborn would surely deter me from my studies. Plus, knowing Kash would be home would make me want to stay home more often.

I clicked my phone to voicemail for the third time. It was Leyanna, and she told me she really need to talk to me. Plus, she wanted to go shopping, and I just wasn't in the mood. Being with Kash right now was my main priority, and anything after that came second.

"Whose call you keep clicking, Princess?" Kash asked as he took a break and sat on the edge of the hospital bed.

"Leyanna. She wants to do some shopping and talk about something," I replied.

"I'm straight; go be with your friend," he encouraged, and I shook my head no. I'd almost lost Kash, and I'd be damned if I was shopping in a mall like nothing happened. Leyanna didn't almost lose Benji, so she didn't understand how it felt to almost lose the love of your life.

"No, I want to be here. I'm tired of y'all trying to make me do what I don't wanna do. I'm good, baby," I assured him, and he laughed.

"You sure?"

"Yes. Now take your heavy ass son," I laughed and handed over our son to him. He held him and kissed him on the cheeks.

"The hell you feeding him?" he joked and acted like he was weighing him with his hands.

"Formula and breast milk. Your mother said to get him used to both because I'm not going to want to breastfeed forever."

"Them breasts still perky and big though." He smirked and licked his lips.

"You're so nasty." I giggled.

He placed our son in the car seat and reached for my hand. I grabbed it, and he pulled me in the hospital bed with him. "You know you're my entire world, right?"

"You tell me all the time, baby." I kissed him on the lips and ran my hands through his hair. "You don't know how much it hurt me that we almost lost you." I kissed him on the lips once again.

"I'm here now, and I'm not going anywhere anytime soon." He kissed me on the forehead, and I laid in the bed with him.

It felt good to lay on Kash's chest and spend this time with him. Almost losing him hadn't been easy, and I felt like I was losing my mind sometimes. I needed him here for me.

6

KASH

BRRRINGG! ***BRRRING!***

THE ALARM CLOCK SOUNDED OFF, and Chyna stayed asleep. She didn't wince or wake up with the sound of the annoying ass alarm clock. I was released from the hospital last night. I told the staff I didn't want to be released in the daytime. I didn't want anyone to know I was alive, or home for that matter. I planned to lay low and see how shit was going down in the street. Today was Chyna's first day back at school. I knew she didn't want to go to school or anywhere else. When I laid down last night, she threw herself on top of me and made sure I didn't move. I could tell this was the best sleep she had gotten since I got shot.

"Princess, it's time to get up." I nudged her, and she mumbled and got more comfortable into the pillows.

I walked to the bathroom to take a piss and take care of my morning hygiene. I heard the bedroom door open, and my mother crept inside. She was in her housecoat, and her hair was tied down.

"Good morning, babies. I brought Kashmere to see his daddy," she said and carried my son in her arms.

My mother was sent from heaven, and I appreciated everything she did. She did the morning feedings for Lil' Kash at night and made sure Chyna ate for the day. She had held this family down, and I wasn't so sure that Chyna would have been able to all alone.

"Why you call him Kashmere, Mama? You know his name just Kash, right?" I laughed and kissed her on the cheek.

"Well, his skin feels just like that. My little peanut knows his nana only calls him that." She laughed. She looked at her clock and then at Chyna. "Oh Lord. She needs to be up for class. Have you woken her yet?"

"Me *and* that loud ass alarm clock tried."

She walked over to Chyna, who was sleeping wildly. She moved her hair out her face and gently shook her.

"Sweet pea, you need to wake up. I have some breakfast on the stove, so get up. You have class, hunnie." She placed a kiss on her forehead and left the room.

I loved the fact that my mother and Chyna had a bond like that. Chyna loved my parents, and they loved her too. Chyna started moving and stretching. She sat up, and her hair was all over her head.

"Good morning, Princess," I said and walked over to her. She smiled when her eyes laid on me and Lil' Kash.

"Hey, my handsome boys... I have class and don't want to go, babe," she whined and looked at me.

"Nah, you have to go to class. No more excuses. I told your brother I would continue to push you in school. Don't make me out to be a liar, alright?"

She huffed, kissed our son, and stalked to the bathroom. I

laughed at her dramatics and went downstairs. It was still painful to walk, but I tolerated that shit. My mama was downstairs cooking a big ass breakfast and humming to the radio. This shit reminded me of living back home when I was a kid. Nothing changed about how she fixed breakfast.

"Did you wake sleepy pants?" she asked and flipped some pancakes onto the plate.

"Yeah, she's grouchy too. Why you cooking all this, Mama?" I laughed and placed Lil' Kash into the bassinet.

"I have my son alive and well and want to get him back to gaining weight. That hospital slop doesn't put any meat on bones."

I sat down at the table and looked at my phone. I had so many damn messages it wasn't funny. I didn't reply to none of them. I wished my nigga Flex was here with me to handle shit. I didn't have anyone I could truly trust right now. I knew that nigga Tike was as real as they came. His name rang bells, and he didn't bang with anybody. He just rode for himself. I knew his girl worked at Chyna and Ley's shop, so I wanted to holla at her about something. I was sure he wasn't making any bread being solo and staying out the mix. Niggas didn't fuck with him because he was known to put a body down with the quickness. Word on the street was that he had ties to the cops and shit. They helped him out and hid bodies and all that shit for him. I had ties too, but more couldn't hurt.

"I don't have time to eat, so I'll grab some fruit," Chyna said as she came downstairs. Her hair was pulled on top of her head. She had on a pair of leggings, a crop top and sneakers, with her MCM tote bag filled with books.

My mama cut up some fruit, placed it in a plastic bowl, and handed it to her. Chyna hugged her, kissed our son, and placed a kiss on my lips. I got up to walk her out the door. She chirped the alarm to her Audi and hugged me once more.

"I have to stop by the shop and see what's going on there. I'll be home right after," she informed me.

"Keep your eyes open, and call me if you need me," I told her and closed her door. She waved as she pulled out the gates. I watched for a minute longer and nodded for one of my security guards to follow behind her. I wasn't about to send my girl out by herself. Niggas wanted me dead, so they wouldn't hesitate to get at her. If something happened to Chyna, I would have to deal with Benji's crazy ass.

I walked back into the house, and my mother had my plate in front of my place at the table. I grabbed the syrup and poured it over the pancakes and eggs. Just taking a bite of the food had me in heaven. After not eating for so long and then having my first meal be some bland ass food, I was appreciative with food.

"I know a lot has been going on, but when do you and Chy plan on getting married?" My mother sat across from me with her coffee. "I was thinking you guys could get married on a private beach in Key West."

I laughed as I washed down the food with the fresh squeezed juice. "Mama, I just got out the hospital, and things are getting back to normal. I don't want to stress her out about us being married right now."

My mother leaned in and looked at me. "Kairo, with the life you're living, you need a wife. A fiancée, girlfriend, or whatever, is a liability. As your wife, if things goes left, your secrets are safe with her. I love Chyna like a daughter and want you to do right by her and my grandson, but you two are living a dangerous life, and things need to be prepped for the future. Should anything happen, who will get what? Me and your father will be fine, but lawyers will automatically hand all your assets to us. Chy and Baby Kash deserves things too."

My mother had so many points that I couldn't really argue with her logic. Chyna was my fiancée, and I was going to walk down the aisle with her. In real life, I lived a crazy ass life, and at any moment, I could be dead or behind bars. I needed to know that Chyna, as my wife, wouldn't allow them to flip her over and make her talk. As my wife, legally, she wouldn't be able to speak on anything we shared. I almost lost my life once and wanted to make sure she and my son were straight. It reminded me that I needed to change my will and make sure they were squared away.

"That's why you're always in my corner, Mama," I said as I heard my son crying. She started to get up, but I touched her shoulder. "I got him. I'll get him changed, and then I have to handle some stuff for the rest of the day."

"Alright. Just be careful and think about what I said, boy."

"Of course." I smiled.

"You and your son share that same face... Lord, what have I done?" she joked and sipped her coffee.

"It's like that, Mama." I laughed.

I carried my son up to his nursery and laid him on the changing table. He was fussy as fuck, and that diaper was feeling a little heavy. I didn't know what Chyna was feeding his ass, but he was fat as fuck. I changed his diaper, clothes, and picked him up.

"I swear I'm gonna die trying to give you the world," I said, and I rocked him in my arms. His gray eyes stared back at me as I continued to rock him. My son had gray eyes, and I didn't know where he got them from. My father said he got them from his great-grandmother and uncle.

I kissed him as he closed his eyes and went into a light slumber. I placed him down in his crib and closed the door. The baby monitor was on, and we had one in every room in the house. I went to go shower and get ready to hit the streets. I wasn't ready to make my comeback yet, but I wanted shit to be in check when I eventually did.

$$$

I knew for a fact that Tike's girl worked at the shop. She worked damn near every day since they opened, according to Leyanna. She said her man came in once in a while to pick her up. I knew Alyssa was a kept bitch and was used to getting whatever she wanted. Still, I did my research, and all the shit she spit to Leyanna about just working there to pass time was a lie. Money wasn't like it used to be, and Tike was trying to make ends meet. He was good at what he did, but if niggas weren't copping, then what could you do? I sat in the back of the car and watched as we drove into the hood. Shit hadn't changed much, and I spotted a couple of my niggas. The tint was so dark that you couldn't see who was watching from behind, just how I liked it.

"It's been crazy since you've been down, boss," Ro said as he drove. I watched as niggas were busy talking and making sales out in the open. It was like they didn't care that they could get knocked. Nah, that's not how I ran my shit, and I worked hard to get BMS where it was now.

"Shit is pissing me off. Head to the girl's shop," I demanded, and he took off.

I checked my watch and put the hood over my head. Chyna and Leyanna were still in class, so I knew Alyssa would be there —alone. We pulled up to the shop, and I stepped out the car and quickly entered. This brown-skinned chick was bent over picking up clothes out the boxes. I cleared my throat, and she turned and looked at me.

"Kash, right? Hey, I'm Alyssa." She walked over to me and introduced herself. "Chy is still in class, but she promised to come by after," she informed me.

"I know where my girl's at," I replied and took a seat on the couch. She held the item of clothing in her hand and looked at me.

"So you're going to wait?"

"Nah, I'm not here for her."

She waved her hands and backed up. "This isn't that kind of party. Chy is a really good boss, and I would never; plus, I have a man."

"That's exactly who I want you to call and have him meet you here." I laughed. It was refreshing to know that she wasn't that type. Bitches these days didn't have any kind of morals about themselves.

"What for? Do you want to harm him?" Her voice shook with fear.

"Do you really think you'd be standing here if I wanted to get at him? I want to speak to him about something. I know shit isn't what it seems in y'alls life," I hinted.

She sighed and sat on the unopened box.

"I'm so tired from working all these hours. I never see my baby anymore, but Tike says it'll be temporary. I trust him, Kash."

"Call him and tell him to meet you here. I want to speak to him about something," I told her and walked to the back. "Send him to the office when he comes." She got on her phone and made the call that could possibly alter her life—if Tike played along. If not, it was back to the drawing board, and she was back to busting open boxes and stocking the stuff.

Not even an hour later, I saw Tike walk into the shop from the security cameras. Alyssa hugged him and pointed to the back. He looked confused but came to the back. I shut the monitor off and looked toward the door. When the door opened, he peeked his head in.

"I didn't take you as a nigga that liked pink." He chuckled and closed the door behind him. "Word is that you're dead."

"That's why I don't trust what the streets are saying unless I can confirm it myself. The truth is that some pussy niggas from

GB want me dead. I could almost bet that it's Solace, but I can't be too sure."

"What that got to do with me?" He messed with one of his dreads.

"I know you're not getting it like you used to. The streets are making you choose a side to make money. You sticking neutral isn't feeding your daughter or baby moms. I know you don't want her working like this." I flipped the monitor on and turned it on. We watched as Alyssa took her heel off and tossed it. She was frustrated with trying to open a box. I could have told her she needed a box cutter, but what would be the fun in that? I needed her to prove the point I was trying to make.

"I'm not neutral; I don't fuck with GB, and that's a fact. Them niggas don't have regards for anything. I just don't want to be caught in the middle of beef, so I stick to myself."

I messed with the new beard I had grown when I was in the hospital. I liked the shit, so I got it shaped up and kept it.

"Look, I want to take GB down and make those niggas bleed. I've been wanting to since they took Flex away from me. Now, they messing with my life, and I can't let them get away that easy."

"Again, my nigga, what that got to do with me?" Tike questioned.

"I want you to run BMS for me. I know you're the type of nigga that'll get my shit back in line. I don't want to show my face yet. Trust, when I do, bodies will be dropping. I drove through the hood, and those niggas living like the Feds don't exist. Come join BMS, and I'll make sure you'll never regret the decision you made."

He played with his dreads and looked at me. "What you get out this shit?"

"My team getting back on their bully. I need them focused and not wilding out. GB will try to cut the head, which they already think they did. I'm not trying to give them the satisfaction of letting the body fall."

"How much you talking, Kash? I know you a real nigga, which is why I'm even sitting here and contemplating this. I need to know shit will remain the same once I step in and do what you need."

"I'll have a million dropped at your crib this afternoon, and you'll make that much damn near every month. Money is never the issue with me; loyalty is."

"I'm gonna be real with you. Money doesn't buy loyalty, and you know that. I'm loyal to whoever holds me down. If you prove that, you got my loyalty. When you want me to rough these niggas up?"

I slid the keys across the table to him and smirked. "Got a meeting warehouse there and rounded them up. I had my security put the word out. We head over there right now, and I'll watch from my office upstairs."

"You was that sure I would accept?"

"Money talks and bullshit walks. I know them broke ass GB niggas can't afford that shit. That's why they all in my pockets, hating." I chuckled.

He stood up and I walked around the desk. "Good looking, nigga, and let's pray we get this bread."

"Bet."

7

BENJI

I LOOKED toward the door as I finished eating lunch. I heard bags drop and mumbles coming from the foyer. Since I came back from that job in Arizona, shit had been hot and cold between me and Ley. One minute, we were good, and then the next, she was being distant and not wanting to be bothered. I wasn't one to chase pussy, so I allowed her to have some time. In the back of my mind, I couldn't help but wonder what we were doing. I wasn't a nigga that liked to sit around and play games. JoJo was soon about to welcome his second child and was ready to settle down. When he showed me the ring that he planned to propose to Renee with, I couldn't help but to ask what the fuck I was doing wrong?

A wife, family, and love were what I wanted. Since my mother passed, it had just been me, Mookie, and my aunt. I wanted a wife and some kids running around. Losing my mother at a young age forced me to grow up quickly. You would think since Mookie was damn grown and had her own thing, I would want to be wilding out and going wild. Nah, I wanted to settle down and have my own shit too. Leyanna was the person I wanted to share that with, but her ass was playing.

"I can't stand when niggas take things into their own hands," Leyanna vented and walked right by me. She held her purse, laptop, and an iced coffee in her hand.

"Fuck she walking by like I'm not standing here," I muttered and placed my dishes in my sink. I walked into the office where she had sat down and placed her stuff on the table.

"Kash ass is out of line, and you need to speak with him," she pointed at me.

"Oh, so you did see me and decided to ignore me?"

She held her hand up. "Our lights are off because I forgot to pay the bill, so I need to stay here for a few days."

"Why the bill not paid?"

"I freaking forgot, Benji. Sheesh. I've been running the shop, school, and trying to maintain our relationship. I'm busy doing everything, and I go into the shop today, and Kash done allowed Alyssa to quit without warning. I had to close the shop because I have a showroom filled with boxes and things that need to be put away!" she yelled and slammed her books down on the table.

"I'll handle the bill, Ley. You barking on me like I'm responsible... I'll holla at you," I said and turned to walk out the room.

All I wanted to do was lay down, get some sex, and watch movies with her. She seemed always busy, so I didn't push her. The last time I was between her legs was a few weeks ago. I grabbed my keys and headed out the door to go and pay their light bill. I needed to stay away from the crib for a few hours. I jumped in my truck and pulled out of the driveway. I saw Leyanna peeking out the window on the second floor. I shook my head and sped down the block. Shit was becoming real annoying, and I was seeing that I was going to have to step away from her and allow her to come to me when she was ready.

After I finished paying the bill, I headed to JoJo's crib to check on him. I hadn't talked to him since he left my house that day. I pulled up to his condo and killed the engine. The doorman was familiar with my face, so he allowed me upstairs. I knocked on the door and heard Renee yelling for him to answer the door. The door opened, and he nodded, allowing me inside.

"What I owe this visit to?" He locked the door behind me.

I walked into the condo, took a seat on the couch, and looked at the view of Miami Beach. Sometimes, I felt like maybe I should have gotten a condo. Mookie wasn't staying at her crib anymore, so what was holding me there? I was alone most of the time in the crib, so why didn't I just get a condo with a nice ass view. I didn't smoke or drink, but I could see myself sipping something or blowing smoke from a blunt on the balcony.

"Renee cooking. You want some food?"

"Ain't pork, right?"

"Nah, I think she made some chicken and rice," he replied.

"Just give me some rice and salad," I told him and sat back, looking at the game that was on the TV.

He came back with two plates, and Renee followed with a beer. I started to tell her to bring me some water but decided to let loose for once.

"Babe, I'll be in the room. Enjoy, fellas," she said and took her food to the back.

"Y'all handled everything? What's the verdict?"

JoJo had a smirk on his face as he scooped some food into his mouth. "It was a false alarm, so I had her ass get on some birth control. Jolie is enough for right now, and I don't want anymore."

"Makes sense, but remember, she has feelings and gonna want some seeds too, even if you don't want anymore."

"Yeah, yeah... Fuck you doing over here, nigga? How Arizona go?"

"Went to go pay Mookie and Leyanna's electric bill and just ended up here. I... I just don't know what's good with us. Arizona was handled quickly and quietly. You know how that go."

"You and Mook?"

"Nah, Leyanna. I haven't had time to be with Mookie. She too busy under Kash, so I'm gonna let her live. I know her ass better be in school every damn day, though."

"Word. What's going on with Leyanna?"

I scooped some food into my mouth and looked out at the view. "Let's sit outside, nigga. Shit too beautiful not to."

We grabbed our plates and sat outside. I stretched my legs out on the chair and started eating my food. JoJo had a drink and was finishing it before his meal. "What's good with Ley?"

"She in school, working too much, and I fall somewhere at the bottom of her priorities. Then, she be wilding for no reason and thinking she the boss. Fuck kind of shit is that?"

"You know she's headstrong, nigga. Ley ain't about to let you treat or talk to her any way without having an opinion on the matter."

"Ain't the point. I ain't fuck in a minute because she so busy. Some nights, her ass be next door and don't even let a nigga know."

"She trying to get that bread, chicken, and gwap... feel me?" He laughed as he held his stomach.

"I don't know why I even talk to your silly ass."

"Nah, for real. She's trying to be a businesswoman, student, and make time for you. You gotta hand her some slack for trying to hold all of this down."

"Damn, if I wanted to vent to her, I would have stayed at my crib." I snickered.

"Nah, Ley is a good girl for you, and you're having issues because you used to them bitches that jump at your every call."

"Nigga, shut the fuck up." I shoved him and laughed.

He laughed as we ate our food and drank beers on the balcony. When that nigga pulled out the strong shit, I wasn't with it, but somehow, he convinced me to have some shots with him. Shit, you only live once, right?

8

LEYANNA

"COME AND TALK TO ME, I really wanna meet you girl, I really wanna know your name!" I heard screaming outside the bedroom window. *"You look so sexy, you really turn me on... blow my mind every time I see your face, gurllllll!"* the screaming continued.

My eyes glanced at the clock that told me it was two in the morning. I knew I should have been asleep, but I had homework to finish, and I was looking for someone to replace Alyssa.

"The way you dress and walk... it really turns me on!" the terrible singing continued.

I jumped out the bed and ran over to the window where Benji was standing in the front yard singing off key with a bottle of Remy Martin in his hands.

"What the fuck? Benji doesn't drink," I mumbled to myself and ran to put on some clothes to go downstairs. I could see neighbors peeking out their windows just like I was.

Who the hell was he drinking with, and why was he drinking? Benji didn't drink, and that was a known fact. The fact that he was standing outside at two in the morning, singing off key, let me know he wasn't just drinking, but he was fucked up from drinking apparently too much.

"Benji! Get over here!" I harshly whispered from the door. All I had on was a pair of shorts, T-shirt, and no bra.

He was still singing and swigging from the bottle like he didn't hear me. *"The shit I wanna do to you got me all hot and shit!"* he continued to sing, and I sighed.

I winced as I stepped on pebbles that littered the gravel. "Get in the damn house, babe," I begged him.

"What you got waiting on me?" He took another swig from the bottle, and I sighed. It was obvious I had to play into his drunken state to get his ass in the house. Benji towered over me at almost six feet six and weighed over two hundred pounds, so how was I going to get him into the house if I didn't?

"Oh, you wanna know? A little something." I walked seductively into the house and thankfully, he followed behind me.

All he needed was for someone to complain, and he'd have to move. Not that it mattered because I was tired of this little cookie cutter Stepford Wives community. If you didn't have a child or husband leaving in the morning, then you didn't matter. The way the women judged me when I went to the community's gym to work out some nights was ridiculous. While they were sitting in the sauna drinking, I was working out and keeping my body in shape. What killed me the most was that these women were in their later twenties. Kid or not, I wasn't about to make living in this gated community my life. This was part of the reason I didn't want to have children. Things would change, and stuff slowly went from being about myself to everything being about a screaming child. The father would make excuses to get away, and then I would be stuck trying to finish school, run my business, and raise a child.

"Benji! Have you lost your mind?" I snatched the bottle from him soon as his feet stepped over the threshold.

"Give me my shit, Leyanna." He tried to grab it back, but I poured the rest in the sink and set the bottle on the counter. "Fuck you do that for?"

"You don't need to have anything else to drink. Come on. You need to get in the shower. You threw up, Benji?" I asked as I took his hands and walked up to his bathroom.

"Maybe." He let out a hearty laugh, and I almost vomited. This nigga had pieces of his vomit in his beard.

"Yes, you did, and it's in your beard." I pointed to it as I gagged over the bathroom sink.

He dropped his draws, and my eyes couldn't avoid the fact that he was hard. It was standing at attention and waiting for me to sit right on it. We hadn't had sex in a little while, and I missed feeling him inside of me. Was his drinking a call out for me? Was he trying to tell me that he needed me, and I had been abandoning him? Getting wrapped in my own shit happened, and I never noticed those around me, so this probably was a wake-up call for me.

"Where my black soap?" He slurred and walked into the shower stall. I watched as he washed his body and licked my lips.

I couldn't resist anymore, so I stripped out my clothes and peeked my head into the stall. I guess he was watching me because I yelped as he grabbed me up and slammed me against the wall. His dick found shelter in my pussy as I moaned out and grabbed hold of his neck. He was breathing huskily in my ear and kissing me on the neck. My legs wrapped tightly around his waist as he filled me up to capacity.

"Fuck, shit is always tight." He groaned and slapped my ass with his free hand. He switched walls and placed my back against the one with the rainforest shower head. The water sprinkled down on us. My hair along with his beard and dreads were soaking wet. It didn't matter that I'd just got my hair done last week; this shit felt like everything, and Benji was putting it down —like always.

I screamed as I moved up and down his pole and winced when I felt him going further into me. Pain was pleasure, and this pain was pleasing the hell out of me.

"Baby, harder!" I screamed into his ear and then bit it. He took a seat on the shower bench and let me do my thing. The way I bounced on his shit and the grip he had on my waist let me know that I was doing my job the correct way.

Making time for Benji had to become a priority and needed to be added as one of the top ones. It was so easy to get consumed in my life and just take advantage that he was going to be here when I was done. Benji wasn't the type to go out and find pussy, so that gave me a sigh of relief. However, he was a good man and deserved for me to pay more attention than I did to him. Chy was busy with Kash and the baby, so I knew she wasn't checking on her brother as often.

"I love you, Wiz." He groaned and slapped my ass.

"How much, baby?" I wanted to know.

"You already know the answer to that." He slurred and slapped me on the ass.

I threw my head back and moaned as he sucked on my breasts and screamed out. This was what I needed to feel from my man. "I know, I know!" I screamed and bounced on his dick.

My body became tense, and I felt Benji's grip tighten on my ass as I slammed myself into him. "Shit, cum for me," he demanded, and my juices released all down his dick and legs. My body felt limp as I fell into his hands. Benji came a few seconds later and washed my body when he was finished.

"I need more of that," I whispered when he carried me into the bedroom. There was no need for me to put pajamas on because I knew he was going to come for seconds. He was drunk, and Benji could never just go one round when it came to me.

"Don't ask for something your ass can't handle," he warned me. My legs crossed his, and I laid my head on his bare chest.

"We need to make more time like this, Benji." I looked up at him, and he looked down at me with low eyes. He was still drunk, yet I prayed that it would sink into his mental. The fact remained that we needed to spend more time together.

$$$

"HOW YOU FEELING THIS MORNING, BABE?" I questioned when Benji dragged himself out of the room to pray. He said a combination of groans and went to his rug.

As soon as he kneeled down at that rug, I knew not to bother him until he was finished. While he prayed, I continued to make his breakfast. It was turkey everything in this damn house. He had turkey sausage, bacon, and even got damn turkey loaf. Who ate meatloaf when it was turkey?

"I don't want any food," his husky voice sounded as he got up from his rug.

"Somebody wanted to be a drunk and get pissy drunk. Do you even remember last night?"

"Fucking you? Yeah, I always remember that." He laid his head on the kitchen table.

I kissed him on the head and placed his food down beside him. After cooking his breakfast, he wasn't about to waste my time or food. "Aww, look how sweet you are. What are we doing today? I feel like we don't hang out, babe."

"Shit, I wanna sleep. My head is fucked up," he complained.

"So Netflix and chill?"

"I don't give a fuck. I'm about to go lay down and go to sleep for the day."

Since he was out drinking, I was going to cut him some slack and allow him to sleep for the day. I figured I'd get Chyna out the house so she could hang with me. All she was concerned with was Baby Kash, big Kash, and school. The shop wasn't even a main concern anymore, which bothered me a little. If we were going to open a business together, then it should have been both of us on the same page.

"I think I'm going to hang with Chy today."

He raised his head up long enough to hear about his infamous Mookie and what she was up to. "Fuck Mookie up to? She doesn't call or shit," he complained.

"You know her mind is only on Kash since he woke up. We just got to give her time, and she'll come around," I suggested, and he waved me off.

"Going to sleep," he grumbled and walked back upstairs to go to sleep.

I guess he wasn't here for the whole Mookie speech. It probably bothered him because before Kash stepped into Chyna's life, Benji and JoJo were the men she looked to for comfort and to feel safe. Now she was engaged to and had a baby with Kash and looked to him for everything.

"Thanks for wasting my time!" I yelled back.

"Wrap it up."

Rolling my eyes, I placed foil around his plate and placed it in the microwave. I grabbed my cell phone and sat on the couch while waiting for Chyna to answer her phone. It was so hard to get her on the phone these days. If it didn't have to do with Kash, the baby, or herself, she didn't make time for it. I wanted to pull her card about not checking on her brother often. I understood that she felt that Kash was the love of her life, but didn't I matter? She never came home anymore, and I couldn't keep her on the phone to save my life.

"Hey, what's up, Ley?" Chyna answered after the twentieth ring.

"Let's do lunch or something," I suggested.

I could already hear the hesitation in her voice before she even spoke. "I have the baby, and Kash has therapy this afternoon."

"Bring the baby," I told her.

"Uh, Ley, I can't right now. I need to be here for Kash right now."

"Fine," I said and ended the call before she could say something else.

It pissed me off that I couldn't even hang with my friend because she was so consumed with her life. I understood that she had her son and things changed for her right now. We weren't college girls with dreams of opening a boutique like a few months ago. Chyna was engaged with a baby. I was worried about my education and making sure this boutique was perfect. After sitting for a few minutes, I went upstairs and found Benji on the phone.

"I thought you were supposed to be sleep?" I questioned, and he held his finger up to silence me.

"Bet," was all he said before he ended the call with the caller. I didn't have to be a rocket scientist to understand what just went on.

"For how long?"

"I turned it down," he said and looked at me while laying back on the bed. "You just gonna get pissed. I could turn down this one; ain't paying that much."

"Why don't you just get out the business, Benji?"

"Because I got a family to provide for; that's why, Ley."

I understood his mother died and this was how he provided for Chyna and himself. Yet, they were straight, and he didn't have to do this anymore. I didn't want to wake up in the middle of the night to a call or knock on the door telling me that Benji was arrested or even worse, killed. It was cool when we were just talking, but now I was all in and in love with Benji. I wanted to be with him for long haul, despite his old school values.

"I'm not about to argue about this shit again." He sighed and turned over.

"I'm going home," I told him and grabbed my books and laptop and headed out the door. Between him and his sister, I was feeling more alone than ever.

9

TIKE

"FUCK IS ALL OF Y'ALL DOING?" I barked when I walked through the warehouse. The meeting that Kash had set up, I decided to dead that shit. If he wanted me to run shit, then I had to do it my way—only.

Just like he promised, he delivered that bread to the crib. Alyssa didn't wait before she started breaking it up and counting that shit for me. Right there on our kitchen table, counters, and some on the stove was one million dollars in neatly stacked money. When I squared all my bills and shit away, I made sure to get that meeting back up, and today was the day. I had to watch them for a couple days before I approached them, and some of the shit I saw pissed me the fuck off. These niggas didn't give a fuck about this organization that Kash built from the ground up. They showed up on the block whenever they wanted, and money wasn't being brought to be counted. I wouldn't be surprised if niggas wasn't skimming off the top, to be honest.

"Tike, what the fuck you doing here?" one of his knucklehead niggas asked. First of all, I didn't fuck with niggas for them to know my name.

"How the fuck you know me?"

"Nigga, you one of those names that ring bells along with Kash's name."

I waved his ass off and waited for everybody to take a seat. When those niggas continued to chat like I wasn't sitting at the head of this table, I took my gun out and shot shorty that spoke to me when I walked in. It was nothing personal, but I was here to let niggas know I wasn't a joke.

"Argghh! What the fuck, man!" He winced in pain. It was a fucking flesh wound, and he was screaming and crying. I aimed for the back of his chair so that the bullet could graze his ass, and he was in here crying and shit.

"Y'all report to me for all things BMS. The shit I've seen is fucking pussy and uncalled for. This is a business, and if you don't act like it, then you can walk the fuck out the door." I sat down in the chair and looked each of them in the eyes. "Y'all on the block whenever you want, niggas ain't doing checks in the traps, and money hasn't been reported or counted. Where the money?"

They must have all thought that Kash was dead and the money was fair game. Kash had more than enough product, and it didn't look like these niggas needed to re-up anytime soon. Each of them looked at each other, and no one bothered to speak.

"How the fuck you think you're about to run BMS? You don't bang with either sides," a short and fat ass nigga spoke up. I didn't bother to waste a bullet on his fat ass because the whopper he was consuming was already killing him slowly.

"Here's two things about me. First, I don't give a fuck about y'alls opinion, and secondly, I do what the fuck I want and when I want to."

"This nigga is funny if he thinks I'm answering to him." Another one laughed and continued to drink his cognac. Here it was, early morning, and these niggas were so worried about drinking and getting smart with me.

"Clear them out," I said, and my team walked through the door and put bullets in all of their heads.

"Boss, what you want me to do with this place?"

"Burn it to the ground," I said and sparked a blunt. Ro, Kash's driver, was waiting and opened the door for me. I was usually never chauffeured around, yet I could admit I could get used to this shit.

"Where we heading?"

"To the new warehouse; you know where, right?"

"Always the first to know. We'll be there soon," he said as he closed my door and got into the driver's seat.

Can you pick up milk? Alyssa sent me a text message, and I laughed. She knew I didn't know when I was going to come home, so she made silly requests just so she could see me for a quick minute before I ran back out into the street.

Bet, I'll bring on my way to the club
Thanks!

Since Kash made it possible where she didn't need to work anymore, she stayed home and took care of the crib. She was ready to get back shopping and spending the dough I earned. I never had an issue with Alyssa spending bread. For as long as I remembered, she held us down and never complained. Our income was always up and down, so I wanted to save the bread for a bit longer before spending it on crazy shit we wanted. One week, we could be eating lobster, steak, and sipping champagne, and the next, we would be eating ramen noodles with sink water. So can you blame me for being a little hesitant with the money?

"The boss has invited you to a BBQ at his house tomorrow afternoon. Bring your wife and daughter," Ro said and looked at me through the rearview window.

"Oh, word? I ain't never been to his crib. Where he live?"

"I'll be there to pick you and your family up at one in the afternoon." He ignored my question.

"Bet."

It was silence until we arrived at the new warehouse. Down in Lemon City, there were nothing but empty warehouses scattered around. It was nothing to find one, buy it, and then conduct business out of it. Ro opened the door, and I hopped out while jogging into the building. My team was already there and waiting for me when I arrived. Those niggas were beasts on dirt bikes and knew all the back streets of Miami.

"They in the room," my right-hand, Zo, said.

"Bet. You ready?"

"For sure."

I walked into the room, and it was a bunch of different niggas from different parts of Florida. Kash's men had become lazy and comfortable. I never wanted a nigga to become comfortable with the line of work we did. He always had to be on his feet and running shit like the cops were watching him.

"If you never heard of BMS, you've been living under a rock, and that may be a good thing... I haven't decided. You all been picked to come here and become part of a team that's all about the money and supplying the best to Miami. If you fuck up, you might as well call your moms and tell her bye. If you do your shit in the streets, then you'll be rewarded. I always want you to move like the Feds are ten steps behind you."

"How will we clap back when niggas try us?" a tall man asked in the back. I could see in his eyes that he was about to put in work.

"You'll be supplied with guns that will be switched every week. Come back here, and you'll have a new gun every week. If you don't, if there's a body on that gun and you get knocked, don't call us for a lawyer or shit. Matter fact, just delete our number out your phone. As for phones, if y'all motherfuckas call me on something other than these phones, I'll kill you myself." I stopped and allowed Zo to hand out the trap phones. "Those will be switched daily, not as often as the guns, but damn near the same time. Don't go hitting y'all bitches on these phones. This phone is to speak to each other and me, that's all!" I slammed my hand down on the table.

"Product and traps?" another man questioned.

I already had a good feeling about these niggas, and that was good for their sake. Instead of asking dumb questions, these niggas wanted to know all the necessities of being a street boss.

"Traps will have no more than four niggas in the crib. Each trap has a basement on the side of the house. I don't want to pull through and see all types of bust heads chilling in front of the shit. Women, come in," I called out, and a few women walked through the door.

"Who the fuck are they?"

The question caused me to laugh because this was a little test. I wanted to see if these niggas would be distracted by the women. Instead, they looked tight that they were even standing here.

"Each of them will be living in the house and cooking your work. Once your work is delivered, there is no need for it to move out the crib unless it's in a bust head's hand. I don't care how y'all make it look to the neighbors, but y'all better not make the shit look suspicious."

"What you mean?" the tall nigga asked. He seemed to be the one with all the questions. It wasn't on no shady shit either; he looked like he was really learning from all of this.

"I don't care if y'all gotta act like their brothers, husband, niggas, or side niggas. Make that shit happen and make money. No one is supposed to know about these trap houses. One man will be responsible for delivering the product to the hood to be sold. Music and loud activity isn't allowed because this is a fucking job. You'll be paid every week from the mailbox with envelopes with your names on them. Any issues, you come to me and me only. Don't pass shit along to anybody unless it's me. Feel me?"

"We got you," they all said in unison.

"Bet. Go get situated. Zo will let y'all know who is going where," I said, and was once again on my way out. I needed to stop by my crib before I made some further moves.

10

CHYNA

"YOU GONNA HELP Mama cook for the cookout?" Kash groaned in my ear as he rubbed my body under the covers. The room felt like an ice box from the central air. Neither of us could sleep if the room wasn't cold. Thankfully, the baby had his own room because he would be freezing in here. My cold toes rubbed against him as he kissed me on the neck.

"Are you sure you want to have a cookout, Kash?" I questioned. Leyanna was still pissed because he let Alyssa quit.

She couldn't wait until she got me on the phone to complain about how being with Benji had made her ass uptight and always working. With school being hard and trying to be the best mother I could, I didn't have room for the shop. Kash told me that I should just let her run the shop and still make money from it. With everything going on, I felt like my time needed to be split between the baby and school.

"Yeah, I want to chill and relax with everybody. That a crime?"

"You know it's August and hot as hell, right?" I questioned

and got out of the bed. My cashmere robe was waiting for me as I wrapped it around my cold body.

"Princess, we live in Miami. The weather is already scalding," he shot back, and I put my hands up in surrender. If I didn't, he would go on and on about why he should have this cookout. It would be nice to see my brother since I hadn't spoken to or seen him in a few weeks.

"You're right. I forget sometimes. Blame me living on the east coast most of my life." I laughed and went into the bathroom.

I ran my shower and washed my hair as I thought about my son and Kash. You ever love something so much that it hurt? That was how I felt whenever I laid eyes on my baby boy. Almost losing Kash made me want to spend every waking moment with him. It helped that he was home all the time. Honestly, I thought I'd become spoiled with him being home more. He claimed that he would be back out in the streets soon, and not to depend on him being home. My heart hurt hearing him say those words to me. I almost lost him once, and I'd be damned if I did again.

"Princess, Mama wants to know if you'll run by the store?" Kash came into the bathroom to empty his bladder.

"Umm, yeah. Let me just get changed real quick," I told him and quickly rinsed my body and hair.

Here I was, spoiled as hell from both my brothers and boyfriend. What nineteen-year-old owned a boutique, Audi, and her own house that she didn't even stay at? At Kash's house, I had my own salon in the basement with a walk-in closet filled with designer clothes. At any moment, I could tell either one of them no, and they'd listen to me. Still, I wasn't satisfied because I worried for both me and my son. After losing my mother, I was deathly scared of losing Benji and JoJo, and now I had to worry about Kash.

Settling on a pair of white jeans shorts, tank top, and a pair of Nike sneakers, I brushed my hair into a bouncy ponytail and headed downstairs. Kash and his mother were sitting at the kitchen table talking when I kissed her and kissed him.

"You look cute, baby girl," Tamar complimented, and I smiled.

"Thank you, Mama. What you need from the store?"

"Oh, you don't need to go anymore. Kash sent Ro to get what I need. Have you fed the baby yet?" she questioned.

"I thought you needed me to go to the store. I'll go and do that right now."

Baby Kash was lying in his bassinet snoozing when I entered his bedroom. I loved the fact that his room felt so peaceful whenever I entered it. It made me feel like my issues weren't as big as I portrayed them to be. Scooping him out of the bassinet, I sat down in the rocking chair to breastfeed him. Leyanna warned me that she heard it was painful. Still, I wanted our son to have the best nutrition, so I sucked it up and got the job done. On the plus side, I lost weight from breastfeeding, and that made it all worth it.

"He don't waste no time getting on that breast." Kash stood in the doorway and chuckled.

"Uh huh. He's so greedy, baby," I whined and laughed.

"He better give me my woman back soon." He smirked and walked further into the room. "Princess, what you thinking?"

The reason I loved Kash was because he always wanted to know what was on my mind. If I was feeling a certain way, it wasn't too long until Kash knew something was bothering me. Being with an older man, I learned that relationships weren't about keeping your feelings hidden from each other. If he wasn't feeling something, he told me, and vice versa.

"Just worried about you, that's all," I admitted.

He sighed and sat between my legs as I breastfed our son. His hands started rubbing my thighs as I rocked in the chair. "I told you about that, though," he tried to reason.

"Just because you tell me something doesn't mean that's what I'll do, babe. I'm literally scared for your life." My voice started to crack.

He turned around and looked at me as I wiped the tears that came down my eyes. Just that quick, I was bawling like a big ass baby. Whenever we spoke about this, I couldn't help but to have tears in my eyes. Kash was almost taken from us the day his son was born. Who the fuck is that heartless? He had to realize that the streets didn't have love for nobody, and it was time that he stepped back from it.

"Princess, I got a team that'll protect me. I'm not gonna be out there like that, but I need to let niggas know I'm not to be fucked with," he tried to explain, and I held up my hand. Flipping my son over my shoulder, I started to burp him.

"I don't want to hear it, Kash. Protect you how?" I managed to laugh through the tears. "Like your last team? You're not understanding that I thought I almost lost you, babe."

When I heard that faint little burp, I got up and placed Baby Kash back down to finish his little cat nap. "I was caught off guard, Chyna. Shit like that won't happen again, and you got my word." He hopped up and grabbed my hand before I could leave the room.

"It doesn't matter what I think, Kairo. You're going to do what you want, and I can't do anything about it. I just pray that me and your son are on your mind when making decisions." My legs couldn't carry me fast enough out the room. The tears were threatening to fall again, and I was tired of crying.

$$$

Everyone had arrived at the cookout and was having a good time. Kash's parents invited some of their friends to have some drinks and tasty food. Tamar really did her thing with the spread of food we were all grubbing on. Kash was sitting and talking with JoJo, Benji, and Tike, while all the ladies sat under the canopy and sipped our drinks. He kept trying to corner me into every tight space to talk, but I maneuvered out of the space and headed back out to the backyard. It bugged the shit out of me because I knew what I was getting myself into before I got into it. Still, I was human and worried about my fiancé and my only child. Could you really blame me for that?

"I appreciate y'all for inviting us," Alyssa thanked us again. She was acting all nervous because Leyanna was throwing her shade.

"Ley, just tell the girl how you feel," I called her out, and she rolled her eyes.

Leyanna turned and faced Alyssa with a smirk fixed upon her face. "I think you're fucked up for leaving the store without at least letting me know. You left the store with a mess that I have to clean up now."

"You're right. I was fucked up and should have called to let you know everything. I... I was just excited about not having to work and being able to be home when my daughter got home," Alyssa explained, and as a mother, I could relate.

"Well, that shit pissed me off and left me in a fucked up position," she continued.

Sipping from my water bottle, I laughed at the way Leyanna was acting. She saw me laugh and burst out in a laughing fit of her own. "Y'all both are crazy." Alyssa joined in on the laughter.

"No, both of y'all are crazy," I corrected her while laughing.

Alyssa looked to be happy with Tike, and if she was happy, then who was I to hold a grudge? Leyanna, on the other hand, had pulled her cell phone out and started typing on it.

"We're relaxing, Ley. Leave work alone for a few hours," I pleaded, and she looked up at me. "Please, Ley."

Pushing her phone into the front pocket of her purse, she sighed. "Fine."

Being that I just delivered a baby and lost some weight, I wasn't as confident as Alyssa and Leyanna, who took off their cover-ups and stood up to spray suntan lotion on themselves. With a cover-up and a one piece, I still wasn't that confident yet. My body changed after having my son, and it was something I struggled to remind myself of.

"Benjiiiiii! You better not!" Leyanna screamed when Benji came behind her and threw her over his shoulder. She was laughing and hitting his back as carried her to the pool. "Chy!" she screamed and tried to reach for me.

"Hold your nose!" I yelled and laughed hard as hell.

Benji jumped into the pool with both of them. Leyanna was fighting to get to the top of the water and screamed when she did. "I swear I'm gonna kill you!" she screamed and started trying to dunk him in the water.

Benji loved to swim, so he kept dunking her and getting free feels. When she had enough, she allowed him to hold her and swim her to the pool's edge. She stomped back over to the canopy with this smirk on her face.

"Ugh, I can't stand your damn brother." She exhaled and sat down on the chair.

"Yeah, alright. You love that man." I continued to tease her until I felt my whole chair lift in the air.

Leyanna held her hand over her mouth. "Oh, your shit about to be worse than mine."

"Put me down!" I screamed and turned carefully to see Kash holding the chair up. "Please, Kasssshhhhh!" I dragged my words. The last thing I wanted was this nigga throwing me in the pool with the chair.

"Tell me you love me," he demanded, and I folded my arms.

When he started walking with the chair, I unfolded my arms

quickly. "Alright, alright!" I screamed and hollered. "I love you, baby!" I hollered, and he put the chair down.

Slowly, he placed the chair back in its place. "Now, give me a kiss."

"Hell no," I protested, and his ass grabbed the back of the chair, and I stopped him. "Sorry, sorry." I laughed and gave him a kiss.

Everyone seemed to think this shit was funny, even Benji. He never laughed, and he was laughing and kicking back with a soda in his hands. Leyanna told me about his drunk little behavior. When she told me that this fool was singing outside the house off key, I almost wished she recorded it for me. He still didn't know that she told me what happened.

"Fuck both of y'all hoes!" I spat and flipped them the middle finger.

"Sorry, but I just got these bundles put in and didn't want to get them wet." Alyssa laughed and picked her drink.

Kash went over back with the guys, and I sighed a breath of relief. Thankfully, he didn't dump my ass in the pool. The last thing I wanted to do was fish myself out the damn pool. The guys continued to talk business, and we sat and enjoyed the drinks and views. I drank virgin drinks, since I had to breastfeed and Benji claimed I wasn't old enough. My birthday was next month, and I couldn't wait.

"So, I don't know what to do for our anniversary... Can you believe it's going to be a year we been together?"

"A year, a baby, and a ring," Leyanna commented. "Damn, y'all was fucking for four months before you got pregnant?"

"Yeah, and I ended up with a damn ring. He knew he better had locked this down... What should I do?"

"Take a trip and fuck the shit out of him. Always works for Tike," Alyssa suggested.

Tike's ass looked like he was a freak and demanded sex on the regular. Kash liked when I fucked him, yet he also liked shit with meaning. Me dressing in lingerie was cute to him, but he liked to really go overboard with gifts.

"Kash isn't like that; we can fuck in the room all day, but we both like to do more when going away, especially with a new baby; we want to have fun."

"I'll watch the baby if you need me to," Leyanna offered.

"Bitch, you just trying to be nice. His nana will be watching him," I told her, and she exhaled.

"Gurl, I didn't know what to do with a newborn baby."

I laughed as we continued to sip on our drinks. It was going to be a year since me and Kash got together, so I was excited to do something. With all that we'd been going through, it was going to be nice to get away with just the two of us. Benji's ass was going to question if my school stuff was taken care of before going away, but he had to realize that I had a child now. He couldn't continue to treat me like I was his child.

11

KASH

"WHY YOU OVER there acting like that, Princess?" I questioned as she sulked on the bed. Her feet were pulled under legs and her arms folded.

My princess always looked good as fuck when she had an attitude. Her pouty lips were always poked out with her eyes narrowed and hands crossed. It didn't help that she had a pair of boy shorts and a sports bra on. The baby was beside her in the bassinet, and she had school books sprawled onto the bed. The TV was on some shit she loved to watch.

"Baby, you know why I'm mad," she whined and kept her hands crossed as she looked over at our son.

Placing my sneakers down on the floor, I walked over to the bed and sat down beside her. "Princess, don't act like that." I nudged her and tried to pull her into my arms.

She resisted at first, and then, just like putty, she melted in my hands. Shit had been running smooth with Tike and the new niggas. When he told me he bodied all the niggas that I used to run with for BMS, I thought the nigga was joking until I saw the warehouse on the news torched in flames. The cops were saying that they believed a massacre took place inside with all of the bones they'd found so far. Tike's crazy ass had killed the whole BMS and started over. It wasn't like I fucked with any of those niggas since Flex passed. Tonight, Tike invited me to some party that he was invited to. I felt like tonight was the night to make my appearance so that niggas knew I wasn't dead. That nigga Solace was going to see me in the flesh when I stepped out tonight. It was only a matter of time before that nigga got his; I wasn't in a rush either. I just wanted to fuck with that nigga before I popped his ass.

"Why do you have to go out tonight? I thought today was family day." She pulled away from me and lifted our son out the bassinet. He started to fuss, but she kissed him a few times on the neck.

"Chy, you know I gotta handle business. Sitting around with you and the baby is cool, but you already know how I get my money."

"Yeah, you get your money from having others work for you. You never have to get your hands dirty, Kash!" She raised her voice a little bit.

"Princess, I gotta head out... I'll see you when I get home," I promised and kissed her on the lips.

She continued to hold our son and looked at me slipping my feet into my kicks. I looked in the mirror real quick and went to give her a kiss on the lips. She moved her face and my lips landed on her cheek. Shit pissed me off because she knew I was just trying to handle business.

"You ready, Ro?" I asked as he opened the door and I hopped in. Clubs weren't really my scene before I got shot. I went only out a few times because Flex always liked to pick up girls. The one time he convinced me to go, I had a good ass time because I met Chyna.

"Yeah, Boss... Lemon City?" I nodded my head, and he headed out the gates to head to the club.

It took thirty minutes to get to the club. Bitches and niggas were everywhere trying to get in. The bouncers were using their desperate behavior to their advantage. Some chicks were promising head and shit that should have made them embarrassed to even say. Still, they were slipping inside like flies with smiles on their face. Ro hopped out and opened the door for me. As soon as my sneakers hit the pavement, Tike came out the club and dabbed me up.

"Finally got you out of your castle," he joked and dabbed me.

"Chy not fucking with me, so let's get this shit going so I can head home," I replied and followed him into the club.

Although it was the hood, the club's layout wasn't too bad. It was only one floor, but there were sections roped off for the VIP section. "Champions" by Kanye West and Gucci Mane was blasting through the club. The light shimmered off my gold chains as I walked through the partygoers.

"Kash, I thought you were dead." One of the chicks that used to suck my dick touched my shoulder.

"Saw a ghost?" I laughed and hugged her briefly before heading to the back where our section was. Tike was dapping niggas left and right as we made it to the section.

"Kash in the building. What up?" the DJ said and nodded his head to me. I put my hands up and walked through the velvet robes. Drinks, women, and the crew was already waiting for us.

"This the boss; everything goes by me before it gets to him!" Tike yelled over the music as each man gave me a head nod.

"Handle business, stay loyal, and you'll be paid—cheers." I held up the cup that Tike handed me, and they followed suit.

"There that nigga Solace go." Tike nodded his head at Solace walking through the club. My eyes followed him to his VIP section. I guess he felt like someone was staring at him and looked up. That was when his eyes met mine, and the nigga looked like he saw a ghost. All I could do was smirk and offer a head nod.

"He's gonna get his soon as fuck." I grabbed the bottle and took a swig out of it. I was never the type to be front and center, dancing on women. More than likely, if I was in a club, my ass was on the couch with a bottle and woman topping me off. Now that I had my princess, none of the old shit mattered anymore. Getting home to her and my son was the most important thing to me.

Her tripping off me going probably scared the shit out of her. Being worried if I was going to make it home to her or not had become a legit concern for her, and I hated that shit. She changed from being careless and only worrying about school and how much shopping she was going to do for the day. My princess still had those spoiled qualities about her, but I could sense that she had matured since all of this shit went down. I didn't know when the last time was she went out and shopped for herself. It was all about our son when she did go shopping. I had to get my baby back to herself and to stop worrying about me, because I could handle myself. From what it seemed, I had some niggas willing to lay their lives on the line. Tike had shit back up running, and the money was rolling back in.

"Hey, so how you been?" the chick that used to top me off sat down and asked. Her name was Veronica, and she was cool.

"Chilling and taking care of my family," I shot back.

"Family? When did that happen?" She shifted her head to one side and smiled. It wasn't a jealous smile; she looked genuinely shocked.

"Got a seed and fiancée. Happened last year and been the best shit that happened to a nigga."

"The streets haven't been the same in your absence, Kash."

"Appreciate it. What you doing out?"

I knew for a fact that she worked a million jobs and could

never get off to top me off when I needed her. Now she was in the club chilling like she didn't have a million damn jobs.

"Off tonight, and I'm only really working one job now. I've met someone." She blushed when she mentioned whoever the dude was.

"That's what up. He taking care of you?"

"For the most part, he does. Enough about our own shit; let's turn up and head home to our lovers in the morning." She giggled and grabbed my arm, pulling me up.

"Bet." I put my feet on the couch and sat on the back piece of the couch while she danced. My eyes kept skimming my phone, hoping that my Princess would hit me up. The drinks were starting to make me feel buzzed, which I hadn't felt in a minute. Tike and his boys sipped their one drink and allowed me to turn up. My eyes weren't even paying attention to Solace, because if that nigga jumped at me, I was going to finish his ass this time. I let loose and allowed my niggas to guard me while me and Veronica turned up. The king was back!

$$$

The sun beat me home before I could even walk over the threshold of our house. As soon as I made it inside, I heard shit being moved around in the kitchen. When I heard my princess's voice, I went into the kitchen to see what she was doing. When I walked into the kitchen, she had Baby Kash on the table in his car seat with a few bags next to the kitchen table.

"Shit, forgot I moved them there," she mumbled as she retrieved her car keys out the island drawer.

"What the fuck is this, Princess?" I barked, and she looked up at me. Her eyes were red and looked as if she was crying.

"Going home. I think it's time for me to be there for a bit." She moved around the counter and grabbed our son's car seat.

"You are home—What the fuck is this, Chyna!" I yelled and followed her to the car. She opened the back door and leaned in to strap the car seat to the base.

"You decided to stay out all night and leave me to worry, so this isn't my home anymore... Stay here while I grab the bags," she demanded like I was going to listen. I grabbed my son into my arms and followed her back into the crib.

Chyna grabbed a few bags and struggled to the car as I followed her back outside.

"You acting like I was staying out because I wanted to, Princess. I had to handle some business and got caught up."

Shit, who would have thought that I would be arguing with my baby? The last thing I wanted her to think was that I was out in the streets because I wanted to be. Coming home and seeing her with our son moving back home did something to me, and it pissed me off.

"You had a choice, Kairo!" she yelled. "Do you think sitting by your side while you recovered wasn't hard? Instead of enjoying being a new mother with my son and fiancé, I was neglecting my baby, sitting with your dumb ass all day, every day!" she dropped the bags and screamed.

"Prince—"

"Save the shit, Kairo. I'm sick of this, and it just started. You almost lost your life and don't give a damn about keeping the one you were spared." She picked the bags back up and put them in the back of the car.

"You 'fuckin crazy if you think you leaving with my son."

"Give me my baby, Kash!" she screamed and snatched him away from me. She kissed him and gently placed him in the car. "I'll be home until you get some sense in your head." She hopped in her car and pulled off. She honked a bunch of times so the guards could open the gates, and sped out.

This shit was already stressing me the fuck out, and I hadn't even gotten my hands dirty yet. Last night was a one-time thing, and I wasn't about to be in any parties anytime soon. Chyna needed to understand that this was the life I lived. What she expected? For me to sit back and act like a nigga didn't try and take my life? Nah, that wasn't me, and it would never be. I needed for her to be supportive instead of beefing about me going out and coming home in the morning. She already knew I wasn't worried about any other bitches. It was about Chyna and my son, and that was all that mattered to me.

I felt bad for lying to Chyna about last night. I had every expectation of handling business and dropped the ball. I ended up drinking and turning up with Veronica all night. We didn't fuck or no shit like that, because she had her nigga and I had Chyna. We ended up going to some after hour spot and getting some food before we split ways and headed home. If Princess knew that I was out with another woman, she would be leaving my ass for good, except it wasn't like that with me and Vee.

"You sent someone to follow her?" I asked one of my security guards, and he nodded his head. She could be mad at me all she wanted. One thing I didn't play about was her and my son's safety, so she was going to be followed by security. Last time, someone tried to murk her because she was driving in my whip. I wasn't about to make the same mistake twice.

12

LEYANNA

"BENJI, we need to do something instead of sitting in the house today," I complained and flopped over the couch.

Benji didn't bother to answer me because he was praying. I knew it was disrespectful to talk to him while he shared this moment with Allah, yet I was bored and tired of not doing anything together. When I was busy with my work and school-work, he complained and felt like I wasn't being there for him. He never actually came out and said it to me, but I knew he was feeling it.

"You disrespectful as shit," he mumbled as he got up from his carpet. I followed behind him as he walked upstairs to his bedroom.

"I'm sorry. I didn't mean to blurt it out right then and there," I apologized and sat on the edge of the bed.

He was in the closet getting things together for his shower. "What you wanna do, Ley?"

Scrolling down my phone, I looked up with a goofy smile on my face. "Can we do this booze cruise?" I clapped my hands together and looked up at him, hopeful. Benji hadn't picked up a drink since he was singing outside at two in the morning. He had a few beers at the BBQ, but that wasn't anything major.

"Ughh!" We both turned our heads and looked at the window. Benji was the first to walk to the window and open it to stick his head out.

"Mookie, what the fuck you doing?" he yelled out the window.

"Moving back home, Benji. What it look like!" I heard her scream back, and I ran downstairs.

I was moving so fast that I didn't realize that I had forgot my phone on the bed and had no shoes on. Chyna was moving bags to the front of the house and mumbling to herself. I don't know what the fuck happened with her and Kash.

"What happened? Why you home, and how long are you staying?" I shot each question after the other. I was just so hype that she was home—in our home.

"Until Kash gets his life together. Can you grab the baby?" she asked and carried the rest of the bags into the house.

Benji came out the house a few minutes later, tying his dreads on top of his head. "What he do?"

"Relax, Benji. He didn't do anything to me, Christ," Chyna snapped as she walked into the kitchen. She looked in the fridge and slammed the door shut. "There's no food?"

"I'm never here, so why would I fill the house?" I shot back.

It was evident that she had a little attitude from whatever happened with her and Kash. "I know, I'm just... never mind."

"Me and Benji will head to the store and get the stuff you need for the baby. Shower, get the baby settled, and don't worry."

"I'm gonna drag the bassinet into your room." Benji jogged up the stairs to handle that for Chyna.

"We'll talk when I come back," I told her, and she gave me a weak smile.

Benji went into his house and grabbed our keys before we

headed to the supermarket. I sat back in the seat and looked as Benji played with his favorite dread. He always messed with it when something was bothering him.

"What's wrong, baby?" I questioned, and he looked at me before he continued driving.

"Ain't shit wrong with me. You good?"

"Stop bullshitting me, Benji. Something is wrong with you, so tell me," I probed.

He touched my thigh and continued driving. "Gotta job to do tomorrow."

"Where?"

"Back in New York," he replied.

"I have a few days off from school. I can come with you."

The face he made almost made me laugh. It was as if he wanted to laugh and then slap the shit out of me for offering to come. "Ley, why the fuck you think I would let you come with me? Me and JoJo got this."

I sat back in the chair and looked out the window as the scenery passed by me. "I'm tripping; I have to work anyway."

"Now you about to try and make shit up." He laughed and shook his head as he drove.

My head snapped and looked at him. "Actually, I have to work and fix what Kash destroyed. Have your little New York killing spree, and have fun with it." I smirked and crossed my arms.

Benji laughed and put his hand on my lap as we drove to the supermarket. Our fights were always petty and ended up with him apologizing, or me admitting that I was acting a bit crazy. He pulled into the parking lot and got out to open the door for me. He reached for my hand, and it fit perfectly into his huge hand. Swinging my Chanel bag over my shoulder, we made our way into the supermarket to get some food.

"Might as well get some shit for my crib too." He grabbed an extra shopping cart and bumped my ass with it. "Shit jiggling right." He licked his lips and tried to palm it. Mind you, there were children and a whole family looking at us.

"Babe, stop being a weirdo and let's get food. You cooking tonight?"

He picked up some puff popcorn that he liked to eat. To me, it tasted like Styrofoam, yet Benji fucked up at least a bag in one sitting.

"Mookie back home, so I'll cook over y'alls crib."

"Fine, but we don't want nothing healthy, Benji," I warned and picked up some cooking oil and moved toward the baby aisle.

There were a million things for babies, and if I didn't know what Chyna liked to use for Baby Kash, I would be lost. She always loved the feel and smell of Huggies, so I grabbed a few boxes of those. Baby Kash had sensitive skin, so he had to get the wipes that were made for just that and had no smell. Chyna didn't play about her son having any kind of rashes, so I didn't even need to pick that up.

"Babies eating better than me." Benji chuckled as he showed me the baby food.

I pushed my cart over to his and laughed as I read the label. "Does Chy having a baby make you want to have one?" It was a valid question. Benji had expressed before that he wanted to be married and have children.

"Sometimes, but I know we gonna have an argument about the shit," he admitted. "When you're ready, then we'll have one."

"I don't want you to hold out on something that you could have because of me, Benji."

He looked at me confused. "What the fuck you want me to do, Ley? Want me to go get a chick pregnant so you can be satisfied? There's no way for us to both get what we want without hurting the other."

"You want children and a wife, Benji. That's not where I am

right now, and I don't think I will get there for a few years. In a few years, you can wait, and I'll still not want to have kids or get married. Where does that leave you?"

He didn't bother to answer me as he pushed the cart down the aisle. Watching his hands grip the handle of the shopping cart, I could tell he was upset. Part of me wanted to continue the conversation, but I left it alone—for now.

"You know what, Ley? Maybe I'll go get a bitch pregnant while I wait for your ass," he turned and snapped on me.

I was shocked that he would even say something like that to me. Was I wrong because I wanted to put myself first for once? A child was going to hold me back, just like it was for Chyna. While she was all smiles and giggles with Kash, she was slacking and having to put in extra work just to keep up with class. Not to mention our shop; she didn't even come by or check in on things.

"You know what? You can go and get a million bitches pregnant, but this chick won't be one. I get you want a wife and family, and I want those same things. Still, I want to give myself time before jumping into that with you. You know the life you live, so let's not even front like you don't."

"Who fronting?" he barked, and people in the aisle were rushing out the aisle with whatever they picked up.

A big black man standing over me with his dreads hanging wild was intimidating, yet I knew Benji wouldn't hurt someone he cared about.

"Let's get the food and go home." I rolled my eyes and pushed my cart by him. He mumbled something behind my back and followed behind me. What was supposed to be a peaceful shopping trip turned into a tense one. No one said anything to the other, and when we got into the car, it was even quieter.

$$$

I decided to stay home after our fight. Benji helped get the bags into the house and then disappeared into his house. Since he didn't have any words for me, I was going to give him his space and allow him to chill the hell out. He had mentioned kids when we first met, and I knew that's what he wanted. Still, I had the right to tell him that wasn't where I was right now. Being his wife was one thing, but having kids was another. Kids changed your life, and I wasn't ready to alter my life right now. Everything that was supposed to happen for me was finally happening for me. We had a business, I was in school, and was finally in a semi-healthy relationship. Why did he want to complicate things right now?

"Why you looking like that?" Chyna walked into the room with Baby Kash in her arms. She took a seat on my bed and started burping him.

Sighing, I looked at her as tears rushed to my eyes. This was so frustrating, and all I wanted to do was be in Benji's arms, not arguing before he left for this job in New York.

"We got into an argument about babies and marriage. Benji wants kids and marriage, and I don't right now."

Chyna shook her head and laughed. "Is this over me and my baby?" She kissed her son's cheek.

"Chy, I don't know. He's been speaking about babies and stuff before you had the baby. I mean, I want all those things eventually, yet right now isn't the time for that. What, I'm gonna send Benji to our kid's school for career day?"

She touched my arm as I vented my frustration. "You think Baby Kash will be able to bring his father to career day? Sometimes, things are out of our control, and that's how it is with Benji. He's been doing this, and he's not going to let you come in and try to make him change."

"I just want to know that he'll come back to me when he's finished. His field of work isn't guaranteed."

"It isn't, but refusing to give your hand in marriage or have kids with him doesn't make it any better."

"You're just used to this because he's been doing this since y'all mothers died. Me? I couldn't get used to this no matter how much I tried," I told her.

"You're going to mess your relationship up if you don't. If you don't, then you're going to lose out on a good man."

Sighing, I didn't have anything else to say about it. I wanted Benji to stop, but I couldn't control what this grown ass man did. At the end of the day, I had to respect what he was going to do and pray that he would come home each time. As far as kids, that wasn't a subject of discussion right now. School and the boutique were the center of my attention right now.

"Anyway, you need to start coming to the shop more." I pulled her card about her not coming to the shop.

"Yeah, I'll make more time to come," she promised, and I laughed because she was lying her ass off. I missed Benji and was gonna make time to speak with him. We both needed to cool off before trying to have a conversation.

13

CHYNA

HERE I WAS, trying to plan something romantic, and Kash goes and pisses me off. I was pacing the floor of my bedroom pissed that I packed my son up and left his house. According to him, it was our home, but when he decided to step out the door and head to the club, it pissed me off. The whole night and into the morning, I was up and worried about him. Anything could have happened to him, and he was acting like I was wrong for my feelings. I was so paranoid that I called hospitals, his parents, and even the police stations asking about him; then, he walks into the house early in the morning screaming about what I can or cannot do. When he didn't answer my call at three in the morning, I packed up some things and tried to leave, yet the guards at the gate wouldn't let me go until the sun came up. Now I knew that was a load of bullshit, and they were waiting for Kash to bring his ass in the house.

It had been two days since I left Kash's house, and my phone hadn't stopped ringing. He left countless voicemails and texted me a million times. He had to understand that I felt like I lost myself when I thought he was gone. He had tubes and everything attached to him, and that was my view for the month and a half he was unconscious. Every time he stepped out the house, I worried for his safety. Someone wanted him dead, and when they found out that he was alive, they would be gunning for his head. Where would that leave me and his son?

The doorbell rang, and I checked in on my son, who was sleeping, before walking downstairs to open the door. Right when I touched the door handle, Baby Kash started screaming over the baby monitor. It was as if he missed his daddy because all he did was cry morning, noon, and night since we got back to my place. His room here looked nothing like the one back at his father's house.

"Oh hell, what the fuck do you want?" I sighed and left the door open to cater to my screaming son.

If someone would have warned me to keep my legs closed, I would have. Being nineteen with a baby and trying to juggle all that I had going on, stressed me the hell out; then to have a hard-headed fiancé who didn't give a damn about how you felt was the icing on the cake.

"I can't see my son, Princess?" I heard Kash say behind me.

"You can; just wait downstairs. I didn't invite you up here, baby," I replied.

He smirked and then tried to grab my ass. "You know you love me because you can't stop calling me baby."

"It's a force of habit, Kash." I laughed and handed him his son.

He took him in his hands and sat down on my bed as he rocked our son. I knew he couldn't be hungry because we had just finished a feeding. He simply wanted to be rocked just like his nana rocked him all the time.

"When you coming back home?"

Messing with the things on my dresser, I tried to avoid

answering his question. Maybe staying at his house full-time was a bit much, and I needed to stay home.

"Not anytime soon. I think it's good for me to be home right now. Benji pays a mortgage for this house, and the least I could do is stay in it."

"Bullshit, Chyna." He called my bluff and laid back on the bed. "If you won't come home, then I'll stay right here."

"You're not staying here, Kairo!" I yelled his government name. For some reason, he couldn't stand when I used it. The only time I used it was when I was really upset. Any other time, he was baby or babe to me.

"Like fuck I'm not," he countered and laid our son next to him.

"Ugh, you're so stubborn and annoying," I whined and climbed into the bed next to him. He put our son on his chest and laughed as I laid on his stomach.

He ran his hands through my hair and laughed. "You so spoiled, Princess. What you want?"

"What do you mean what I want?" I asked and messed with his Gucci belt that he sported.

"I fucked up and need to make it up to you. What you want?"

"I want a yacht and for you to settle down and leave the streets alone. Or at least step back and let Tike handle his business."

"How you know about Tike?"

"You don't think I listen while you're on the phone, babe? I'm not dead, just supposed to be sleep."

"All I can tell you is that I'll try, and that's all I can give right about now." He sighed.

I took Baby Kash from him and placed him in his crib in the next room. He fidgeted for a few and then settled into the crib for a slumber. Walking slowly back into the bedroom, I took my boy shorts off and straddled Kash. I didn't need to even touch him for his dick to get hard.

"Mookie, where you at?" Benji yelled through the house. I got off of Kash and pulled my pants back on.

I closed the door behind me and walked downstairs, where Benji was in the kitchen raiding the fridge.

"Shit is nasty as fuck," he grumbled and closed the fridge.

"Why you screaming when I just got your nephew back to sleep?" I sighed and folded my arms.

The way he looked me up and down, I just knew the questions were about to come.

"What you doing home in the middle of the day?"

"They allowed me to take my classes back online. I only have to go to classes on Friday," I explained and plopped on the couch. "Why you screaming my name?"

"I wanna make Leyanna my wife," he revealed, and I looked at him with wide eyes.

"You wanna marry Leyanna?" I got excited and started to jump up and down. I was so excited I almost forgot about Kash waiting upstairs for me.

"Where she at anyway?" he questioned.

"You don't know where she's at?"

"She ain't fucking with me since I left to go to New York and didn't tell her. We been beefing and shit, and I think this is what will shut her ass up."

All I could do was sigh because Leyanna was adamant about not getting married or having kids. "Ley is not in the same space as you, Benji. She doesn't want to get married with what you do, and I don't blame her." I sided with Leyanna.

For as long as I could remember, this was what Benji did. He was in and out, and it was like he didn't take lives for a living. It afforded us the ability to live comfortably and never have to depend on people. Growing up with whatever I wanted and being spoiled by both JoJo and Benji, it didn't matter either way to me. Almost losing Kash made me see the dark side of the business. The dark side of the business had always been there; I just chose to ignore it. If something was to ever happen to Benji, I would for sure lose my mind.

"I want her to tell me that to my face while looking at this." He passed me a velvet red box.

It was as if Kash was asking me to marry him all over again. My hands were all shaking like this was my ring or something. When I finally opened the box, there was a gorgeous ring sitting in the middle. I had to squint because it had so many diamonds, including the huge center rock. If Leyanna told Benji no, she was a dumb ass for sure, and I would surely take it.

"Dang, this ring is beautiful, Benji." He had to pry it out my hand.

"She need to realize this shit is what I do, Mookie. I wanna provide for her, and she trying to do it on her own," he complained.

"Bee Bee, she wants to be an independent woman. You honestly can't fault her for that. You can still provide for her, just not financially like you want."

He shook his head and messed with his dreads. "Shit too fuckin' annoying. That's why the fuck I stay to myself," he vented.

We both turned and saw Kash coming down the stairs, holding our son. He dapped Benji up and handed me our son. "I gotta head out real quick," he said and walked toward the door.

"Don't bring your ass back here, Kash. I'm not doing this with you!" I yelled and startled my son in the process.

Benji just looked at both of us and shook his head. He grabbed his nephew and kissed him on his forehead. "Fuck is wrong with y'all?"

"All he wants to do is run the streets like he didn't just almost die. I can't go through that again, Benji." My voice cracked, and I wiped my tears. These damn hormones were still raging and caused me to cry at the drop of a hat.

Benji touched my arm and looked at me. "Mookie, you already know what's it like to be with a street nigga. You asking him to stop running the streets is like asking him to stop breathing."

"When we met, he wa—"

"When y'all met, his shit wasn't under attack. If he sits back now, they'll think that nigga is soft as shit."

"His son's life and mine should mean something to him. Kash isn't broke and can afford to step away from this, just like you. Y'all just choose to be selfish as shit."

"Ain't got shit to do with being selfish. Money don't grow on trees, Mookie. If I stopped doing what I do, where would we be? Somewhere broke while you messing with some lame nigga. Although I have my doubts with Kash, the nigga still willing to take care of you and your seed."

I gently took Baby Kash from Benji and walked toward the stairs. "Go home, Benji. Talking to you is like talking to a wall," I told him and walked upstairs to my room, where I slammed the door. Placing my son in the bed, I climbed next to him and thought about all that Benji was speaking about.

14

BENJI

MOOKIE WAS TRIPPING, so I decided to bounce and go see what was good with Leyanna. I knew if she had class, she would be out by now and heading to their shop. Ley's ass lived in that damn boutique, and if she wasn't inside of it, she was talking about the shit nonstop. I understood where she came from with being independent, yet I still wanted to take care of her. Leyanna meant the world to me, and I would die trying to give her fine ass the world. She saw beyond my money and my occupation. She respected me as her man, and when I made moves for us, she followed. Lately, she'd been tripping about what I did and how she didn't want to be married with kids while I still fulfilled hits on people. If I didn't catch her ass riding the nigga I was supposed to kill, she wouldn't have even known what I did for a living.

I pulled up to the boutique, and her truck was parked right in front. The lights in the store were off, so I knew she was in the office. This shit was real nice and could make them some bread in the long run. Too bad Mookie was too busy worrying about Kash to run her own damn business. Her ass had better not be lying about taking online classes because I'd put my foot in her ass if she was.

"Benji, what are you doing here?" I heard Leyanna's voice from behind me.

I turned and looked at her carrying donuts and coffee in her hands. "Came to see you; what you up to, Wiz?"

She smiled while opening the shop and stepped in. "Lock it behind you. Girls been waiting for it to open because of the window displays." She smirked to herself. "I've been good. What about you?"

"I ain't been too good, been sick lately." She looked at me concerned before I elaborated. "Sick without you."

I watched as she exhaled and shook her head. "Enough with the jokes. What do you really want?"

"You."

She set the donuts and coffee down before walking over to me. "Why are we fighting?"

I wanted to tell her it was her fault why we were beefing. She was the one who caught an attitude because I chose to pop niggas and get paid for it. If it wasn't for me, this whole little boutique wouldn't have been possible. Leyanna needed to realize that even if she didn't like what I did, she had to respect the shit.

"It don't even matter. Stop beefing, Wiz."

She laughed as she hugged and kissed me. "Everything is always so laid back with you." She giggled.

"Life's stressful enough. Why we gotta add more to it? What you doing in here?" I looked around and it looked damn near completed.

"Just trying to make it perfect. I even hired a girl after Kash called himself being a boss and letting an employee quit."

"Oh yeah? When she start?"

"Tomorrow. The store is opening for the first time since Alyssa quit." She got excited when she revealed that.

"Proud of y'all," I said, and her face changed as she looked at me.

"Y'all?"

"You and Mookie."

"No, me. I've done this entire thing on my own. Ordering clothes, making sure contractors got things together correctly, and stocking almost everything myself. Why does Chyna get credit for this?"

The conversation went left when all I did was just show that I was proud of them. I wasn't keeping up with what they chose to do with this boutique. All I did was transfer money into their little business account. I got along with Kash because he was my nephew's father and Chyna was so in love with him. With the secret he was holding, it was only a matter of time before Chyna found out and wanted nothing to do with him. This boutique was a source of income for both her and Leyanna.

"Chill. All I said was I'm proud. You need to talk to Chyna about how you feeling."

"I'm not feeling anyway," she tried to lie, and I looked at her with a blank stare as she exhaled. "I've just been doing all the work while Chyna gets to be mommy, fiancée, and do her school work. I know her son is her first priority, yet she gets help from Tamar and still doesn't come to the boutique. Since moving back home, all she does is stay in the house, do her work, and watch TV while waiting for Kash to call her. How is that fair to me?"

"Talk to her, Ley."

She nodded her head and rolled her eyes because she knew I was right. Holding all this shit in wasn't about to make things any better. In the past, I had always had Mookie's back and would go to the war over her. Leyanna was my queen, so I had to learn how to stay mutual in their little beef.

"I will, eventually. What you doing today?"

I smirked because I had come to check her and take her out

for her birthday next week. Birthdays weren't my thing, and I told her that; still, I had to make an effort because she got so excited over that shit.

"Chillin', and I came to give you some stuff," I said and pulled out a packet of papers.

She grabbed them hesitantly while looking at me through squinted eyes.

"Benji, you didn't!" she screamed and jumped into my arms. I held her up while she slapped me all in my face with the damn papers. "We're going to Paris?"

I smiled because she kept going on and on about how she wanted to visit there. To make that shit happen for her made me feel proud. Who else could make her dream come true but me?

"You excited?"

"Yes!" she screamed and jumped down while trying to catch her breath. "Next week? What?" She continued to jump around more excited than before.

"You know I've been wanting to go there since forever. I can see if I can take some time off from school and have Chyna make sure the shop is opened and stuff."

"Bet. You can take off for the rest of the day?"

"Why?"

"I need you." I touched her ass, and she turned around into my arms. Fucking the shit out of her was on my mental. Leyanna's ass been staying at her and Mookie's crib. She was long overdue for some dick, and I wanted some pussy—now. I wasn't a nigga that begged, yet right about now, I was ready to beg her for the gold she held between her legs.

"I need to do a few more things, then I can leave. How about I meet you back at the house?" she suggested, and I had no choice but to agree, unless I was about to fuck her in the office. The thought didn't sound too bad right about now.

"I'm 'bout to go check JoJo," I said and kissed her before leaving the store.

$$$

JoJo had told me to come through to his crib because he had to talk to me about something. When I arrived, Renee was holding a sleepy and fussy Jolie. It amazed me how Renee stepped into the position of being so nurturing toward another woman's child. You couldn't tell that Jolie wasn't her child when she spent the week with them. Jolie respected and listened to her more than JoJo's ass. He thought everything was a joke when disciplining her.

"Where he at?" I asked as I hugged Renee and kissed her on the forehead.

"Hey, Benji. He's on the balcony," she said and disappeared down the hallway. I went into the living room and out onto the balcony where he was sitting.

"What happened? You good?" I asked as I took a seat beside him. He was smoking a blunt and drinking cognac.

"I can't just want to see my brother? We ain't chilled in a minute." He laughed and took a pull of his blunt.

"Shit, I ain't drinking with your ass again. You had me fucked up last time I was over here with you," I joked, thinking about the night I got drunk and went home to Leyanna.

"Ahh, I forgot your ass is a prune. So get high and drunk off this view then." He chuckled.

"How you and Renee?"

"We chilling and still going strong. She really wanna have a baby, and I know because of the way she treats Jolie. She acts like she's her daughter with their matching outfits and shit."

"She's her stepmother, so she might as well be. Jolie over here just as much as she's with Lilly at her crib."

"That's a fact. You and Ley?"

"She stressing about me stepping out the game. I ain't about to leave because she asking me; how I'm gonna eat?"

"She gotta realize this is what the fuck we do. We make our bread and butter from this shit."

I sighed because it was frustrating when Ley was on my case about this shit. We had arguments and stopped talking for a few days over this shit. If she didn't spend her time thinking about and feeling like she had to talk about it, we would be good and wouldn't have any issues. Yet she felt the need to bring the shit up every time we had a free minute.

"You right, but Leyanna is like Mookie, with their hard-headed asses."

"That's why they good friends. How she doing with Kash and shit?" he asked.

"Trying to get themselves back together. Her ass better continue with school if she know what's good for her. Mookie think money grows on trees."

"She probably really do the way we both throw money her way. Mookie spoiled as shit, and Kash don't make it better. He got her ass staying in that castle, and she think she's Queen Sheba."

"Kash didn't have to do that because Mookie already thought her ass was a queen."

"You right." He laughed.

I kicked it with JoJo for a few before I headed home to cook something for me and Leyanna. We didn't have too much alone time, and we were long overdue for some time together.

15

SOLACE

LILLY'S ASS shouldn't have come back to my crib talking that crazy shit. She claimed she came to get the rest of Jolie's shit and then she was out. Well, one thing led to another, and she told me she was pregnant. If that wasn't enough to make a nigga feel like he was about to pass out, she added she was going down to child support to make me pay. That wasn't what pissed me off. It was when she said they'd dig into how I made my money and make me pay her a bunch of money. My fist just collided with her face, and I continued to stomp her the fuck out until she was lying unconscious in the living room. Her face was unrecognizable, and she wasn't pregnant anymore from the damage I did.

I quickly called the police from her cell phone and then dipped out the house. Niggas wasn't about to catch me with this shit. I was pretty sure that she was dead or would be fucked up if she turned out to be alive. Don't threaten me with bullshit and not expect to get your ass handed to you. How did she think that conversation between us would turn out? She thought I was going to be cool and request documentation from all the bust heads that bought work from me? Then sit in court and hand the shit over to the judge? Nah, that wasn't me, and all because she wanted to be greedy for child support for a kid that wasn't even here yet.

Now, if she came to me and told me she was keeping the baby, we could have talked. I wasn't a totally fucked up nigga. If she was adamant about keeping the baby, then I was going to take care of my child. No, Lilly wanted to come in like she had the biggest set of balls and got her shit busted because she came to me like that. The cops were going to want to question me, and I wasn't about to be around. I quickly pulled into the driveway of my lil' mama I had been fucking for a few months. She was loyal and knew her place, which was why she got bumped from her current living residence to this house. Yeah, it was in the hood, and niggas occasionally got crazy, but she didn't complain.

"Hey, baby," she greeted me with these small ass shorts on. I slapped her ass and kissed her in the mouth as I closed the door and locked all the locks. "Somebody chasing you?"

"Nah, nah," I said as I looked around the living room and kitchen. "What you got to eat?"

"I made some chicken and rice. Want some?" she questioned, and I nodded my head as I kicked my clothes off.

Snatching a bag from the bottom cabinet, I put my boots in the bag along with my clothes before going to shower. She was looking at me weird but never asked one question.

"Babe, your food is on the table," she called while I showered.

"Thanks," was all I said as I washed my body of any evidence. I needed to go burn those clothes and shit when I got a chance.

After my shower, I sat in her bed, and she catered to me like a king. That was another reason I came over here often and got her this crib. She knew not to nag and get on my nerves. When I said something, she already knew that was my word, and she had better not go against it.

"I have class tomorrow, so can you drive me?"

"How you been getting to school before that?"

She sighed and sat down beside me. "The bus or cabs if I have the money."

"Aaliyah, you better continue with that shit." I laughed.

She hit me and giggled, but I was dead ass serious. Shorty was cool to fuck because she was in school and was a major freak. She didn't complain when I bought her Jordans or little shit, unlike some of these bitches nowadays. They wanted all the designer shit, and a nigga like me wasn't going to come off the bread for that shit, especially for them. I met her at a party in Lemon City, and she was cool as fuck. She topped me off in the bathroom, and the rest was history. Me and Lilly had gotten into arguments because she would find lipstick on my dick, or I smelled like another woman. Half the time, I wanted to tell her ass that I did smell like another woman, and she sucked my dick good too.

"Whatever. I'm going to finish this school work. Call me if you need me." She sighed and walked out the room.

Her ass wasn't slick; she just wanted to be seen riding in my whip. I wasn't about to be caught up like that with her young ass. Wasn't it enough that I had moved her out the dorms, into a two-bedroom crib? Bitches, man; they were never satisfied with the shit you did for them. I turned the news on and damn near choked on the food I was eating.

This is Channel Six, and we're reporting a home invasion at this residence. A woman was beaten nearly to death in her home. The safe was emptied, and furniture was turned over everywhere. There's no answer as to why this happened or if she was targeted. She's in critical condition now. Her fiancé is nowhere to be found, but a neighbor has said he moved out a few months ago, and it was just she and her daughter. As more news develops, you'll hear it from us first.

I sighed a breath of relief as I thanked that nosy ass bitch of a neighbor. She was watching so hard that she missed a key point. Lilly's ass moved out, and I stayed in my crib. I emptied my safes and turned furniture upside down to make it look like an invasion. It was only a matter of time before they tried to track me down and speak to me. Right now, I was going to lay back because too many people wanted me at one time. Kash wanted my head on a platter. I guess he musta found out that it was me who popped his ass, and now he wanted to return the favor. I was gonna let shit cool down before stepping foot out this crib.

"Aaliyah, go put my whip in the garage!" I yelled and laid back in the comfortable ass bed before knocking out. Kicking Lilly's ass was like cardio or some shit.

16

KASH

CHYNA WAS dead serious when she said she wasn't coming back to the crib. She had been at her crib and wouldn't come to my crib—our crib. She had been over there so long I almost started calling it my crib again. The only bright side was that she allowed me to spend the night with her and the baby. Sleeping alone in the crib wasn't the wave, and it made me miss her more. Being able to wrap my arms around her and be up when she did midnight feedings with our son made me feel better. She still wasn't feeling me being out and leaving in the middle of the night. Solace's ass had dropped off the radar, and GB wasn't worth shit anymore. Niggas from over there were trying to get down with BMS, and I wasn't having that shit. If you could be disloyal to this nigga Solace because shit was going left, then what made me any different?

Half of them niggas, I should put a bullet in their heads for even stepping to Tike about the shit. How the fuck you try and get with the team that you spent all your time trying to take down? How the fuck did that work? Tike had been doing his thing and was worth every penny I paid that nigga. Money was flowing in, and bodies were dropping. Half of GB's customers were knocking on our traps, and shit couldn't be any sweeter. Nah, if I had Solace's body in front of me, begging for his life, shit would have been even sweeter. I couldn't look the other way, this nigga needed to be gone. He tried to take me away from my family and didn't give a fuck about it. Shit wasn't going to be sweet with that nigga at all.

"Where you coming from?" I questioned as Chyna walked into her crib all dressed up like she was coming from smiling in another nigga's face.

"School. Where else would I be coming from?" she spat back and placed her purse down and took her heels off.

"You go to school dressed like that?"

"Yeah. I wanted to look nice today. Why are you even here?" she snapped. Another thing was this attitude she had. Every time she spoke, she had this little smart ass reply for whatever I asked.

"I came by to see what you were up to."

"When you saw I wasn't here, why didn't you leave?" she questioned and pulled her laptop out along with her books.

"Why you acting like that?" I asked and watched her as she walked up the stairs to her room. Waiting a few, I got up and followed her upstairs.

When I got upstairs, she was prepping for a shower. I licked my lips as she took her shirt off and stood with her bra on.

"Kash, stop being a creep," she scolded and tried to push me out the room, but my hands latched onto her hips. I kissed her on the neck and she moaned, feeling my lips on her neck. "Nooo," she moaned.

"You sure? Your body telling me something different," I said and pushed her back into the room. She had on a pair of tight ass jeans that I shimmied down her legs before I pushed her down onto the bed.

For someone who didn't want to be bothered, she seemed all in now with the way her legs were spread on the bed. I dipped my tongue in that shit and slurped like I hadn't had a drink in over two days. The way Chyna's body shivered from the penetration my tongue was doing to her sent chills down my body. Pushing her legs further apart, I was damn near inside of it the way I was eating the shit out of her pussy.

"Tell daddy you like it," I told her, and she tried to form words, but the shaking of her body wouldn't allow her to.

Dropping my pants, I mounted her, and my dick felt like heaven once I was inside of her. Chyna was moaning and scratching my back as I propped one of her legs over my shoulder.

"Shit, right there," I groaned as I continued to fuck the shit out of Chyna. She was screaming and moaning as I gave her the business.

Being inside of her and hearing her scream for me made my dick harder, if that was possible. We had been going through, and being in this room with her while fucking out of frustration made me feel good. Chyna was my baby, and she wasn't going anywhere. This pussy was mine, and there would never be another nigga getting between her legs.

"I'm aboutttt," she moaned.

"Hold it for me. I'm behind you," I demanded, and she did just as I said. Quickly, I pulled back and rammed myself into her, and we both came at the same time.

"Leave, Kash," she mumbled.

"You dead ass gonna continue this petty shit?" I got up, mad that she was still on the same attitude when I walked in here.

"You thought sex was going to change my feelings? I still feel the same way."

"I can't tell from the way you was screaming," I barked back.

She rolled her eyes and looked at me like I hadn't said

anything that mattered to her. "Kash, see your way out," she said before slamming the bathroom door.

My phone buzzed, and it was Tike. He told me it was 911, so I gathered my shit and left. If Tike hadn't told me to meet him, I was prepared to lay in this bed naked as the day I was born. Business called, so I was out the door in under a minute.

17

LEYANNA

I WAS SO EXCITED to be on the way to Paris. This had been a dream of mine, and I couldn't believe that Benji had made it happen for me. After talking to Chyna, she agreed that she would open and close the shop along with keeping an eye on our new employees. With all the money we put into the store, it was about time that we started to make some money back from it. Even though she had the baby and her issues with Kash, she had to dust that off and step up with helping me run the boutique. It had been me doing everything, and I was tired of letting her reap the benefits while I busted my ass to make sure that this business was successful. When she was pregnant, I gave her an excuse and let her rest. Now, she wasn't pregnant, had help with the baby, and had more time than before, so what was her excuse for not stepping up and running the shop?

"Why you over there looking like you're thinking of a master plan or some shit?" Benji asked from his seat.

I sipped the champagne that was provided and laughed. He really went all out with these first-class seats that we were seated in. My laptop was open while my notebook was on the armrest.

"Just thinking about the store. I feel like I forgot to mention something to Chyna." I sighed.

He touched my cheek and looked at me. "You gonna bring up your store the whole trip? 'Cause I can bring up a list of shit I turned down to come on this trip," he hinted.

"Fine, fine. I just want to land already." I looked out the window. The pilot had announced that we were going to land in an hour or so. I was getting restless sitting on this plane for all these hours.

"What you wanna do first when we land?" he questioned and locked his hands with mine. He raised my hand to his lips and kissed it.

Blushing, I looked at him with lust in my eyes. I wanted Benji right here and now. The way he was licking his lips, his dreads were pulled on top of his head, and the smell of his cologne were all contributing factors in me wanting to pull his clothes off right here and now.

"Maybe feel you inside of me." I blushed as the words left my mouth. Benji usually was the one who took control when we had sex. I never had to voice that I wanted him; he always just knew. Me telling him right here on a plane that I wanted to feel him inside of me made me blush and want to cover my face from the way he was looking at me.

"Sip some more of that shit. I want you ready when we land." He smirked and caressed my thighs.

When the flight attendant walked past us, he grabbed the bottle and poured more into my champagne flute. "Stop trying to get me tipsy." I giggled and put the cup to my lips.

Benji couldn't leave it as we were going to fuck when we got off this plane. He slipped his hands under the blanket they provided and messed with my leggings until his hands were inside my pants and panties. Just the touch of his fingers fighting to enter me made me want to moan.

"Shhhh." He reached over and covered my mouth with his, while his hands were still in my pants. I kissed him and moaned in his mouth when his fingers were inside of me. He moved them around and tried to open my legs wider so he could pull them out and push them inside deeper.

"Benj—"

My words were cut off when he pushed deeper inside of me. An 'o' shape occupied my lips as I felt myself about to cum on his fingers. Benji knew what he was doing because he kept smirking and kissing me on the neck. When I finally opened my eyes, an old white lady sitting next to her husband was looking at me mortified. She kept nudging her sleeping husband to look at us.

"She's watching," I whispered in Benji's ear, and he didn't give a fuck. He continued to finger fuck the shit out of me. Looking down at his bulge made me want to fuck the shit out of him. The bathroom was right in front of us, yet people would be watching and wondering why we were in the bathroom together.

"Cum for me." He ignored what I told him, and I focused back on busting this good nut. If this was making my eyes roll in the back of my head, I didn't even want to imagine what the dick was about to feel like.

Benji kissed me again to keep me from screaming out in pleasure, and I came on his fingers. He took them out and sucked his fingers before wiping the saliva off his hands.

"I'm so embarrassed." I leaned my head on his shoulder and laughed. For that lady to be so disturbed, her nosy ass watched the entire time with a shocked expression on her face.

A half an hour later, we landed and went through customs then went to look for our bags. Benji chased the conveyer belt and cursed a few times while grabbing our luggage.

"Getting old, old man," I joked and hit his rock-hard abs. My baby still worked out every morning and was muscular like hell.

"Stop fuckin' with me." He mushed me into my luggage.

Since I overpacked and had about the three suitcases along with a carry-on bag, Benji had almost all our bags. I spotted my name and looked at him with a smirk. There was a chauffeur waiting for us.

"Ms. Griffin," he said as he stepped up.

"Yes," I told him, and he grabbed the bags from me immediately. We walked outside and there was a limo waiting for us. "Babe, you didn't!" I squealed and jumped up and down as I looked at the Hummer limo.

The chauffeur opened the door for me, and I slid inside with Benji right behind me. There were different sorts of liquor and champagne in the back. If you weren't into alcohol, you could grab a soda, juice, or water from the bar as well. There was a blue light inside, and the carpet had the logo of the company on it. Here I was, in another country being treated like a princess. All the nagging I had been doing made me feel bad.

"You didn't have to do all of this, Benji," I said.

He touched my thigh as he laid his head back. "I know what I don't have to do. You live off this birthday shit."

"I wish you would let me do something for your birthdays," I brought up, and he nodded his head.

It sucked when you couldn't do something for someone who gave everyone so much. Birthdays and pretty much any other holiday, Benji didn't celebrate. He did it off the strength of me, and I appreciated him for it. Still, I wanted to be able to plan something for him and for him to actually be excited about it. I guess I should be grateful that he was still willing to do these types of things for me, even if he wasn't feeling them.

"So, what do we have planned for tonight?"

"I got something planned that you're going to like." He smiled, and I leaned my head on him. Being in another country with the love of your life was amazing. I just wanted to take in the country with him and have some down time. If he was able to step away from his work, I could do the same to assure we had an amazing trip filled with sex, shopping, and being a tourist.

$$$

"YOU LOOK BEAUTIFUL AS FUCK, LEY," he complimented when I stepped out of the bathroom. I was dressed in a red sequined dress that stopped at my knees. My heels were nude along with my clutch. My face was beat to perfection, and my hair was pulled into a tight ponytail to give myself a slight face lift. When in doubt, pull your hair into a tight ponytail.

"Thank you, babe." I reached up and kissed him on the lips.

I may have looked fine, but Benji looked sexy as hell. He had on a pair of dress pants that stopped at his ankles and red Gucci loafers with a matching colored shirt. His arm was blinding me with his big face Rolex that was sitting on his arm. His dreads were glistening with coconut oil and tied to the back with a rubber band. His face was even shaped up, thanks to the barber that came to the room earlier. He reached out his hand for me, and I grabbed it. Pulling me into his embrace, I inhaled his scent and accepted the kiss he placed on my red-colored lips.

"You know I love you, right, baby?" he asked me as he looked down into my eyes.

Nodding my head, I touched the side of cheek and kissed him. "I love you too, Benji Johnson," I said.

The knock disrupted us from the intimate moment we were sharing. The attraction was so strong in the room that you could cut it with a knife. Benji gently let me go and went to answer the door.

"Mr. Johnson, your ride has arrived," was all I heard, and then Benji closed the door behind him.

"You ready for dinner?"

Looking at myself in the mirror that decorated the living room in our suite, I grabbed his hand and we left the room.

The hotel we were staying at was gorgeous. We had a top floor suite with a living room, kitchen, and huge bedroom. The tub was right in the bedroom in front of the balcony doors that opened all the way. I planned on opening them up and sexing Benji in a bubble bath. The whole vibe of Paris just made me feel super sexy. We came off the elevator, and valet was standing there with keys in his hands.

"Enjoy dinner, Mr. and Mrs. Johnson," the valet said as Benji held the door open for me. Benji was driving us in a McLaren sports car.

"Babe, I don't doubt you or anything, butttt this isn't America and the streets are different," I reminded him.

"I got this, Ley," he said while concentrating on pulling out from the curb. We pulled off, and he hit the brake hard as hell. "Shit," he muttered to himself.

"We can grab one of these cute taxi things," I offered.

"I'm gonna get us to this damn restaurant," he barked, and I put my hands up in surrender.

If he thought he could get us there, who was I to judge him? Once he got on the right side of the street, we were driving down the streets of Paris in the most exclusive car. My birthday wasn't until tomorrow, yet I felt like today was my day with the way Benji was showing out for me.

It took us thirty minutes to get to the restaurant. The valet took the keys, and Benji helped me out the car. With my arm linked with his, we walked into the restaurant. Benji gave his name, and we were led to an elevator that took us forty floors off the ground. While we waited for the elevator to take us to the floor, we fooled around and kissed. With Chyna stressing me, with school, and Benji working, we hadn't had fun in while. It was so easy for a relationship to go from being all smitten to stressing and not remembering the last time you kissed your man.

"Oh wow, this is beautiful!" My hand flew to my mouth when the elevator door opened. It was a balcony with a table set along with two chairs. The Eiffel Tower was in the background. We were literally going to be eating dinner in front of the Eiffel Tower. He led me to the table and pulled the chair out before going to sit in his.

"I know shit been on the rocks with us lately. You know my goal in life is to keep that smile on your face."

"Aww, babe, you make me smile when you're not making me crazy." I took his hand in mine. "I just want to know that you're safe at all times. You don't think I worry about you?"

The waiter came and poured some champagne into our glasses, and Benji stopped him. "Sparkling water."

"Sure, Mr. Johnson." He politely smiled and went to go get the water Benji requested.

We didn't have to order off the menu because Benji had picked out the menu beforehand. They came by with food and just served us like a queen and a king. The lobster was steamed to perfection, and the shrimp were as big as my hands. I should have known that Benji wouldn't let me be great with some sort of meat or something. The seafood was on point, so I wasn't complaining too much.

"This is what I do to provide for my family, Ley. I need you to understand that I'm doing this because I have to, not because I want to."

"It's looking like you're doing it because you want to. Your sneaker store should pull in enough money."

"We here to celebrate you, not talk about me." He switched the conversation. In a sense, he was right, and we had all the time in the world to speak about that.

"You're right. I appreciate that you brought me here for my birthday."

He reached across and caressed my ring finger while looking me in the eyes. "I love the shit out of you. Being with you opens me to shit that I'm never open to. It feels good having someone who looks out for me," he stated.

I chewed the piece of lobster I had shoved into my mouth and choked it down before responding. "I'm always going to look out for you. You've looked out for me on more than one occasion, babe."

He grabbed my hand, and we walked over to the balcony, where we were standing exactly in front of the Eiffel Tower. He grabbed me around the waist from behind and kissed me on the neck.

"I wanna marry you."

"I know; you tell me all the time."

He turned me around and looked me in the eyes. "No, I really wanna marry you." He opened a box, and there was a gorgeous ring. "You good?" he asked as he held me up.

My legs got weak when I realized that he was asking for my hand in marriage. Benji Johnson wanted to marry me, a college student that didn't have her life all figured out and could be slightly annoying at times. He wanted to make me an honest woman out of me.

"Since I met you, you've been on my mind. I just want to protect you and make sure you're good in life. You don't want kids, and I'm willing to put that aside to make this shit work. One thing I don't see myself doing is not putting a ring on your finger and giving you my last name."

I tried my best to keep the tears away as I listened to him profess his love for me. Hearing how genuine and serious he was about making me his wife, his rib, made me cry more. Benji didn't care about much, yet he showed me I was one of those people he cared about the most.

"Baby." I sniffled and touched his cheek. "I don't know what's in the future for tomorrow, next week, or even next month. If kids are what you want, then in the future, we can have some. I want to travel the world with you, make memories, and enjoy being newlyweds, if you'll have me as your wife." I smiled through the tears.

He slipped that rock on my small finger and picked me up to spin me around. I held onto his neck and kissed him on the lips. "I love you, Leyanna."

"I love you too... We're really engaged, Benji!" I squealed and kissed him on the lips.

The lights on the Eiffel Tower lit up in red as he held me in his arms and we kissed. I talked all that shit about not being his wife or having his kids, and now I couldn't see myself not doing those things for him. The love I held in my heart didn't compare to anyone I'd ever been with. We argued, but what couple didn't? This was forever, and I was going to prove to Benji that I wanted to be with him for eternity.

18

CHYNA

MY BROTHER WAS GETTING MARRIED, and I was so excited for him. Leyanna made him happy, and that was all that mattered. Plus, she was my best friend and business partner, so it was a match made in heaven. When they called me and she screamed on the phone about being engaged, I cried for my brother. My mother would have been so proud to see how we turned out. I wasn't sure she would approve of Benji's occupation or the fact that I got pregnant at nineteen. Still, she would be proud to know I was in college and had my own business. She would also be proud to see that Benji found someone who loved him just as much as I did. Benji deserved someone to love and care for him. Since my mother passed, it had been about me and making sure I was straight. It was never about Benji or how he was coping with everything. Now he had a woman that wanted to know how he was feeling and just had his best interest at heart; I could rest easily.

I swerved in and out of traffic on my way to pick my aunt up from the airport. It was about time she came to see her great nephew. Baby Kash was going on three months, and she had yet to come to visit him. Just in time, I pulled up to arrivals and waited for her to come out of the airport doors. Digging down, I grabbed my ringing cell phone and answered.

"Hey, bro, what's up?" I answered.

"Stressing... Where you at?" JoJo questioned.

I hadn't hung out with my other brother in a little while. Things had been so tense, and now they were calming down. I just wanted us to get reconnected like we once were.

"I'm picking up Auntie from the airport. What happened?"

He sighed. "Lilly's bitch ass nigga beat her bad. She's in the hospital and in real bad condition. I've been hitting Benji all morning, and he hasn't hit me back yet."

"Ohh, he didn't tell you? He's in Paris with Leyanna. They're on their way back tonight," I informed him.

"Shit, he did mention that shit to me. It slipped my mind dealing with this shit. You know she don't have much family beside her moms, but she's sick so she isn't much help," he vented to me.

"Where's Jolie? I'll come get her so she doesn't see Lilly like this," I offered.

My aunt had come out the airport and was standing there waving like a diva. I wasn't paying her no mind because my mind was on my niece and if she was alright. I waved her to the car, and she rolled her eyes and dragged her suitcase over to the car.

"She's with Renee. I've been up here since I was called last night."

"Where's her boyfriend? They arrested him?"

"Nah, don't know where he is. They don't even think it was him because the neighbor said he moved out. I heard them say it was a home invasion gone wrong."

"Bullshit. Lilly has lived down here forever. You really think someone would rob her? She lives in a nice neighborhood too."

"I'm putting money it's her little boyfriend or whatever.

When Benji lands, make sure you call me and let me know. I'm going back in her room now," he told me before we hung up.

My trunk slammed, and my aunt swung the passenger side door open. "What a greeting, Chyna."

"Sorry, Auntie. JoJo's baby mama is in the hospital; she got beat up," I said and looked at her.

"Is Jolie alright? Was she there?"

"No, his girlfriend got her. I'm gonna check on him later on."

"I'll come with you."

"How was the flight?" I changed the topic. It was getting a little depressing, and seeing my aunt was an exciting moment.

"Better, since your baby daddy put me in first class. Where's Benji's bigheaded ass?" she asked as she put her seat belt on.

"In Paris. He's coming back tonight. He got engaged to Leyanna."

My aunt had never met Leyanna, but when we spoke, I told her about her. "What? Benji's getting married?" she asked, so surprised.

"Yep. I can't wait to plan the wedding or whatever they plan on doing."

"How's everything with you and Kash? Oh, and the baby?"

I sighed because things weren't bad; maybe I was just overacting. "I'm still at my place, and he spends the night most nights. Well, when he isn't ripping and running. His mother helps out a lot."

"Y'all close?"

"Tamar is amazing, and I love her. She loves her grandson to death." I smiled, thinking about Tamar's relationship with Baby Kash. There wasn't anything she wouldn't do for her grandbaby. She was miles away from home with her husband to help me and Kash out with our son.

"At least she's somewhat of a mother figure. I always worry that I'm not around enough to help you out with being a mommy," she said. "It's hard to teach someone how to be a mother when you haven't been a mother. Well, in a couple of months, I'll be." She tried to slip the last part in, and I heard her loud and clear.

"You're pregnant?" I laughed as I looked at her. "Somebody finally about to make you their baby mother." I continued to laugh and rubbed her stomach.

"He's married and wants nothing to do with the baby. Me, him, and his wife had a threesome after some party. He must have cum in me because next thing I know, I'm pregnant with his baby."

"That's crazy. What did he say when you told him?"

"Girl, his wife wanted to raise the shit together. She can't have kids or won't have kids; some shit like that. He straight out gave me a thousand dollars to get rid of it."

"Wait, an abortion doesn't cost that much. This a street nigga?"

"Nah, he some politician. I met him and his wife at some bar when I was going to handle some shit for my old boo that was locked up. After speaking to his lawyers all day, I needed me a drink. One thing led to the other, and we ended up in a hotel room fucking each other's brains out. They called me a few times after, and we all fucked again, until I found out I was pregnant."

"You always in some crazy mess, Auntie." I cracked up laughing. Only my aunt would get pregnant after having a threesome. "So you wasn't messing with no one else?"

"Hell no. My dude is in jail for eight years, and that's where my heart is."

"So when he gets out and realize you got a seven or eight-year-old kid, what you gonna say?"

"That my pussy needed some loving. He wants me to wait eight years and not have kids. I was gonna get rid of it and went to do it. Something told me maybe it's time for me to stop being wild and calm down."

"A kid will do that to you."

"You would think after taking y'all in, I would have calmed down. Nope. I went crazier when y'all moved out. It's fucked up how this baby was conceived, but I wanna raise it and love my baby."

"Aww, motherhood is something else. It ain't all cute like those teens on TV brag about. My stomach is flabby, and my vagina feels like it's loose."

"It's all in your head. I was thinking..." She allowed her voice to trail off.

"What were you thinking, Auntie?"

She laughed and looked at me. "About moving to Miami with y'all. I'm all alone, and I'll have to do this pregnancy alone."

"You never need to ask to be around family. I have a spare bedroom, and you can stay with me. Plus, Benji is right next door, and I'm sure Leyanna will be moving out soon."

"Whew! I packed most of all my stuff and was banking on you telling me yes." She laughed, and I looked at her like she was crazy.

"So, you're not going back?"

"Yeah, once in a while and to check on my apartment. I just needed somewhere new and fresh to be. I've been depressed about the baby's father not wanting to be involved, and I just need some new surroundings."

"Benji is probably gonna question you, but you're grown, right?" I laughed because he acted like he was both of our big brother. "You're family, Auntie, and I will be there for you the entire pregnancy."

"Thanks, Chy. I knew I could count on you." She rubbed my cheek, and I smiled.

$$$

After I got my aunt settled in my house and showed her around, I drove over to Kash's house. Tamar had taken Baby Kash to visit Kash's dad. She told me she would be back tomorrow night. Any other mother would have anxiety about being away from their baby for a night. Me, on the other hand, I was happy that my baby would be close to his grandparents. Right now, he was too young, but when he was older and they shared that bond, it would mean so much. The only reason I was coming over was because Kash asked me to.

I figured I had been hard on him lately, and he had to handle his business. It still didn't make me feel any better when he was out at night, and I was home worrying about him. We had to come to some kind of understanding about this, and quick, because I missed being with my baby. He stayed the night over at the house, yet it wasn't the same. We didn't kiss, cuddle, or laugh like we used to, and it was because of me. My ass carried an attitude with him anytime he was around, and I had to realize that wasn't fair to him. Someone tried to take him away from me and his son, and he just wanted to get back at that person.

"I didn't think you would come," he said as he watched me grab my purse off the passenger seat.

"I told you I would, and I'm here... My aunt is in town, and I had to show her my house real quick," I explained to him.

He nodded his head and pulled me into a hug. I could smell his Armani cologne coming off his t-shirt. "Am I going to get to meet her?"

"Of course. She's been talking about meeting you since you upgraded her flight."

We walked into the house, and he closed the door behind us. In the foyer was a woman with two massage tables set up with different oils.

"We been worrying about shit that won't matter in ten years. We need to relax and shit," he told me.

"You being alive matters in ten years, Kairo," I had to remind him.

He laughed and kissed me on the neck. His chin hair brushing against my neck caused goosebumps on my skin. I wore a maxi dress with flip flops, and my skin was tanned from the bright sun rays Miami had to offer. Being that it was the end of August and it was hot as hell, no goosebumps should have been forming on my skin. Kash was the only man that could cause goosebumps to rise on my bare skin.

"I mean, it do, but I don't want you stressing and us always bickering and shit. Baby Kash don't deserve to see that."

"He doesn't, but Kash, I just worry, and it makes me angry. Like you don't care that I care about you."

"Princess, I know you care, and that's part of the reason I want you home in our palace. I don't plan on being on this shit forever. That's why I'm making the moves to leave Tike in charge so we can enjoy life. You hear me?"

"Yes, but you need to pick up your phone when I call you, Kash," I warned, and he laughed before kissing me on the lips.

"I can try. Not all the time am I able to pick up my phone. What I'm gonna tell niggas? Hold on real quick, wifey calling me right now?"

"Ummm, yes. It could be about anything... our son or your parents."

"Ight, I'm gonna try, Princess," he promised as he kissed me on the lips. I knew he was desperate because he kissed my glossy lips, which he hated.

"I don't need try, Kash." I looked at him with my lips pursed. When he was out and doing him, he didn't answer his phone for anything. I could call him until I was blue in the face and wouldn't get a response until he walked his ass in the door. He couldn't do that to me; it wasn't fair. It wasn't fair to leave me worrying because he couldn't take a second to send me a message, voice message, or even a damn telegram.

"Ight. I'll call and let you know where I'm at every hour." He smirked.

"Don't be a smart ass." I rolled my eyes and looked at the lady standing there looking at us. "How she gonna massage both of us?" I questioned since it was only one of her and two massage tables.

"My friend is running a little late," she apologized, and I smiled.

"If you wanted to surprise me, you should have had a stylist come to my salon. My nails are disgusting, and my hair is gross," I complained.

"Stop being like that, Princess. I set this up for you, so go on and change to get this massage," he ordered me.

When Kash raised his voice, I knew not to go against him. It didn't matter that I was pissed at him and he was trying to kiss up to me; when he told me something, he wasn't playing around. I was acting bratty in front of this lady and complaining about something people would kill to have. He had roses littered all under the massage tables and soft music playing. Since he was released, I had been begging him to spend more time with me and not out in the street. He was finally doing that, and I was complaining. I needed to sit, relax, and enjoy this massage while catching up with my man.

I came out of the room in a silk robe and climbed onto the table. The warm oil she used on my back made me moan out like she was sexing me. Kash sat on the other table while watching me and on his phone. The way this woman was rubbing my body, it didn't even matter about Kash being on the phone.

"What's going on with the boutique? A couple of my niggas' girls want to shop there, and it's been closed," he brought up.

"Leyanna went to Paris, and she wanted me to open and close it for our employees. I couldn't be bothered, so I closed it until she came back." I shrugged my shoulders.

"Princess, you know this your business, right?"

"Well, duh, Kash. I just had class and the baby, so I couldn't make it around that way. It ain't like we're hurting for the money." I looked up from the table, and I could tell Kash wanted to say more, yet he didn't want to piss me off again. "Say what you was gonna say, Kash."

"Leyanna seems like she's serious about this. Like, this about to be her entire world. If you not serious, you should give her the option to buy you out, Princess."

"I'm into it. I just didn't have time, Kash." I sighed.

"My mother could have watched the baby. What else you had to do?" he grilled me.

"School."

"So you couldn't go open the shop and get back to school work? I mean, you don't head to school until ten. The store opens at nine, so you couldn't swing by there?" Kash was grilling me like a corner boy that lied about being robbed.

"Isn't this supposed to be relaxing? Quite frankly, you are getting on my nerves and not making this much of relaxation."

"My bad. Continue."

Hearing how he was hounding me about why I didn't do this or that pissed me off. I didn't jump into his business and start trying to run shit like I owned it. Me and Leyanna had a system that worked for us, so who was he to try and question it?

19

BENJI

"WE NEED to figure out this wedding business." Leyanna sat on the bed while I laid back, looking at the ceiling.

The last thing I wanted to do was tell my baby I had to go stay in New York for a few months. This new client wanted someone big dealt with, and this wasn't just a quick trip and then back home. We just got engaged, and I had another month before I was supposed to head to New York and get this handled. I'd done marks without JoJo and been back home in under a day. Still, this one would take a few months, and that was if things went smoothly. JoJo was dealing with Lilly and upset about who had done this to her. If I had to place a bet, it was her man and the same nigga that Kash was checking for.

"When you wanna get married?" I asked her as she leaned next to me with her notepad. Since we got back from Paris a week ago, she had been talking about this wedding nonstop.

"In a year or two," she put the pen near her chin and suggested. I wasn't about to be engaged for a year or two.

"This month; pick a weekend, and we'll make it happen," I told her and tried to turn over to get a quick nap.

"This month? Why the rush?"

"A year is too long. I could have done without the ring. What's an engagement? Being boyfriend and girlfriend with a ring."

"Benji, you truly want to get married this month? What about my parents? You haven't even met my father yet." She shot all these questions and concerns like it mattered.

"All that could be arranged. Tell me what you want, and I'll make it happen."

She looked at me with a shocked expression, and I laughed. "I want a beautiful wedding. I don't want a shotgun wedding, Benji."

"Then beautiful is what you'll have," I told her, and she kissed me on the lips. "This month; don't fuck with me, Ley."

"How are we gonna get everything done in time?" she questioned, not believing that I could have this done.

"Ley, I gotta go to New York for a job. This isn't a little job, and it requires me to live out there for a few months. I already told them I would do the job, so I can't turn back now." I held her hands because she tried to get up from the bed.

"Why, Benji? Is this why you want to be married so quick? Just leave this life alone, baby." She scooted closer to me. "I'll have your babies and anything, just please," she begged.

"I wanna marry you because anything can go wrong in my line of work. Here today and gone tomorrow is what could happen. Mookie is taken care of, along with my aunt. I want to assure that you, as my wife, are taken care of as well."

She sniffled and wiped the tears that slid down her cheek. "So I'm supposed to spend months away from my soon-to-be husband? Can I at least come and visit you?

"Ley, now you know I don—"

"How am I supposed to be away from you for months, Benji?

I can't even fly out to see you, but I'm supposed to be cool with this." She got off the bed and paced the floor.

"Stop all that fuckin' complaining. My life ain't easy and it never has been. This is what the fuck I do, Ley," I barked, and she jumped.

While looking at me, she shook her head with tears coming down her eyes. "I don't get a good vibe about this job." She sobbed.

"I never get a good vibe about any of them, Ley. I murk people for a living," I said, and she shook her head. "Come here, Wiz." I reached for her, and she climbed into my arms.

"I don't want to be without you for months. We should be moving into a home and starting our lives as newlyweds, not being apart."

"All that will happen, and I promise you that... Just trust that I'm gonna handle this job and be on the plane back home to you."

"Promise?"

"Promise. I want you to start house hunting too. I'm done doing this neighborhood shit. Get us something right on the beach. Beach bungalow or some shit."

"A tri-level one, right?" She got excited.

"Whatever you want, just something on the beach." I laughed, and she looked me in the eyes as she played with my dreads. "I love you, Wiz."

"I love you too, Benji." She kissed me and leaned back on me.

We laid in the bed for half the morning before Leyanna got up to clean the crib and catch up on school work. JoJo had been up at the hospital stressing, so I was going to go up there and check on him. When he told me what happened, I couldn't believe someone would do Lilly that way. I thanked Allah that Jolie happened to be with JoJo when it happened and that Lilly's mother found her. Doctors said if no one found her, she would have died on the floor.

After getting dressed, kissing Leyanna, and grabbing some food, I was on my way to the hospital. Halfway there, Mookie hit my line, and I picked up the phone. She had been busy with her own shit, and we hadn't spoken. Since I had been back from Paris, me and Leyanna hadn't left the crib. Call it pre-honeymoon or some shit; we were doing us in different places and positions.

"Hey, Bee Bee, what you doing?" she questioned.

"On my way to the hospital to see how Lilly doing. What's good with you?"

Mookie had been staying to herself lately and hadn't been coming around. I knew she was dealing with her personal shit that she would tell me about when she was ready. Still, I missed my baby sister coming to me for everything. I was her problem solver and handled shit for her. Now Kash did all those things for her, and I was left somewhere down the list for her.

"How's she doing?" She sighed.

"Lilly woke up," I informed her.

"That's good. Has she spoken?"

"No, her voice box was crushed. He was telling me about some medical term they used."

"Wow, I can't believe anyone would do something like that to her. I've been praying for her."

"That's all we can do; she's in my prayers all the time. How you been?"

"School and the baby, pretty much. Me and Kash made up, but I'm still at my place."

"It's crazy you live next door and don't even check on your brother. I'm type hurt, Chy."

She laughed into the phone. I heard my nephew fussing in the background. "You and Leyanna been so locked up in that house that you don't even know Auntie here."

"Oh, word? How long she staying?"

Me and my aunt always butted heads because she was so

free, and I didn't need that shit around Mookie. Yet she was the only one who stepped up and tried to raise us the best she could. I didn't go to bed with shitty clothes and no food, so I was grateful to her for that.

"She's pregnant, Benji," she whispered.

"I know you didn't tell me that Auntie is pregnant?"

"Yeah. She wants to move down here because she wants a fresh start or whatever. I told her she could stay here because I'm always back and forth between here and Kash's house. Plus, it'll just be her and Leyanna half the time."

"Ley 'bout to move out soon," I told her.

"I kind of figured that, but y'all gonna move in together before the wedding? I need to sit down and talk to Leyanna."

"We getting married this month, so find someone that can plan this shit."

"What?" she screamed into the phone. "What the hell do you mean you're getting married this month, Bee Bee?"

"I got some shit that needs to be done, and I want Leyanna to be my wife before I go and do that. You gonna plan it or not?"

"Hell no. I can pass on a planner for you. Y'all need to go get a marriage certificate ASAP, Benji," she told me.

"Ight, I'll do that. I'm gonna stop by your crib and see Auntie so she can meet Leyanna."

"Okay, cool. Later." She ended the call, and I pulled into the hospital parking lot.

After stopping for some flowers and balloons, I headed up to Lilly's room. When I opened the door, there were machines beeping, and JoJo was sitting beside her sleeping. Lilly's eyes were open, and when she saw me, she tried to speak.

"Chill, don't speak. I got these for you," I whispered and showed her the flowers and 'Get Well Soon' balloon. She touched my hand and looked at me.

She looked so bad, and I felt so bad seeing her like this. JoJo jumped up and then calmed down when he noticed that it was me.

"When you get here?"

"Nigga, you think I was standing here with flowers in my hand the whole time?" I tried to joke.

He wiped the sleep out of his eyes and sat up in the chair. After sliding his shoes back on, he went over to Lilly's bedside. He grabbed her hand gently and leaned closely to her face.

"I'm about to speak with Benji real quick. I'll be down the hall," he told her.

She squeezed his hand to let him know that she understood him. We headed out the room and went to the lounge a few doors down. I took a seat across from JoJo and waited for him to vent. We hadn't been around each other like we used to be, but it was because we had our own shit going on. When it came to handling business, we broke away from our personal shit and handled business together.

"How's her mom taking it?"

JoJo sighed and hung his head in his hands as he looked at the floor. "Oh, you didn't hear, she on the fifth floor," he sarcastically said.

"Damn, son."

"Renee been holding down Jolie. When I come home and look at her, it's like I can't even look at her when she asks for her mother."

"You found any word on this nigga?" I referred to the lame ass that did this shit to her. He shook his head no and continued to mess with his hands. "I'm heading back to New York for a few months to handle that job."

"Shit, I forgot about that. I could use that bread right now." He sighed. "What Leyanna think about it?"

"She ain't too happy, but she agreed to marry a nigga before I went."

JoJo's eyes left the floor and looked at me. "Damn, I guess congrats are in order. You serious about her, huh?"

"As a heart attack; she makes me feel like I could do this husband shit. A woman hasn't caught my attention like she has in a long time."

"I hear you, and I'm happy for you, bro. Renee wanna have a baby, and I think I'm ready to give her that."

"Everybody having kids." I chuckled.

"You gonna be next or maybe before me; shit, who knows."

I laughed because Leyanna wasn't about to have no kids right now. She was just on board for our wedding she kept calling a shotgun wedding, so having a kid would make her crazy and start problems. If Allah wanted me to have kids, then I would have kids.

"Nah, she not feeling the mommy train right now. Maybe in a few years."

"I feel you, I feel you."

"Lilly need anything? I can get whatever she need."

"Nah, she good right now. She got good ass insurance, so she straight. Just keep them prayers coming."

"Always, bruh, always. You know me and hospitals don't sit too tight." I got up and dapped him.

"Nah, I appreciate you even coming, for real."

He stood up, and we embraced in a brotherly hug before I left the hospital. Since my mother passed, I couldn't take being in a hospital. Mookie meant so much to me that I went to be there for her after she gave birth to my nephew and when Kash got shot. JoJo was my right-hand, so the least I could do was to check him and see where his head was at. He wanted to kill whoever got in his path, but I could see where he was maturing because of Jolie.

It took me a few before I headed back to Mookie's crib. Her car wasn't parked outside the house, so she was probably with

Kash or something. I let myself in, and my aunt was in the kitchen with a tub of ice cream while something was cooking on the stove.

"Benjiiii!" she yelled and walked over to give me a hug. "I swear, when are you gonna stop growing?" she joked.

"How you been, Auntie?"

She returned back to the counter and took a spoonful of ice cream. "All over the place. This house is gorgeous. Chyna is really living the life, huh?"

"Something like that. She could live the life without a baby and a fiancé too," I muttered, but my aunt was so nosy she heard the words before they even left my lips.

"You still mad about the baby? He's here now, and there's no turning back." She sighed and looked at me.

"I'm not mad, just disappointed. I moved her away from New York to avoid this shit. She struggling to keep up with school work because all of the shit she trying to juggle. When you ask her if she good, she won't tell you she isn't because she trying to be superwoman."

"Sounds just like Carol." She laughed as she spoke about her sister, my mother. "Always trying to do a million and one things instead making sure she's alright first."

"Mookie ain't built for that life, though. I don't know... shit too much." I messed with my hair and looked at the bacon she was putting on paper towels.

"She's growing up, and you can't control her like you once did when y'all was younger. If she's in school, just trust that she'll finish with or without the baby. Tell me about this new fiancée of yours." She smiled.

I couldn't help but to join in and smile too when I thought about Ley. "She's just right. That's all I gotta say."

"So, is she going to convert to Islam?"

Leave it to my aunt to bring up something neither of us had decided on. "We ain't spoke about that yet."

"Hmm, you prepared to celebrate all those holidays you don't celebrate? Christmas, Thanksgiving, and all the extras. 'Cause when y'all have children, they're going to want to celebrate those holidays."

"It's something we need to talk about. I ain't worried. She's open-minded."

"Yeah, until you want her to cover her body from head to toe," she added.

"Why you asking all these questions? Ain't you carrying a child now?" I laughed and looked at her.

"Chyna has a big ass mouth. She told you, didn't she?"

"Who else would tell me? What's up with the baby father?"

"He's not going to be involved. Just me and the baby." She sighed and ate more ice cream. I wanted to ask her why she made bacon if she was eating ice cream.

"You know I got you if anything. I'm not the daddy, but you've been there when I needed you the most, so it's time for me to return the favor."

"Don't make me all emotional, Benji." She fanned her face with her free hand.

I laughed and walked around the counter to hug her. "You know any home we own is yours. Mookie probably gonna be moving out with her man anyway."

"You get along with him?" she asked as we broke our embrace. "I know you're overprotective, but how is you and JoJo's relationship with him?"

What was I supposed to say? That I had to bite my inner cheek when I was around him because he killed your sister? That anytime I thought about it too long, I had to stop because a tear would slide down the side of my cheek. The man who took my mother away from us was now my nephew's father.

"We good," I lied.

Mookie wanted to push us together and make this a happy family, being oblivious to what Kash really did. Yeah, I went and visited him in the hospital and told him I would find some information for him, but why was I going to help him get revenge when it was his karma? I'd been hearing about his warpath in the streets, and all I could do was shake my head. He better had known what he was doing, because once a hair on my sister's head was touched, it was gonna be war, and I couldn't be held responsible for who was dead after the gun smoke cleared.

"Uh huh, I know what that means. You don't like that man. Chyna is bringing me to his place tomorrow. Come along," she suggested.

"Nah, I'm good. You know how to plan a wedding?"

"Ehhh, no... why?"

"Because me and Leyanna getting married this month."

"Why so soon? I haven't even met her," she blurted while trying to choke down the rest of her ice cream.

"Because I'm not about to have a long ass drawn out engagement."

"Can I meet her?"

"Come on. She next door," I told her, and she smiled. She tried to rush upstairs so she could change, and I caught her hand mid-stride.

"Benji, I'm in pajamas. She can't meet me like this."

"Come on. You and Mookie always gotta be on a thousand every day, huh?"

She sulked yet followed me next door. I opened the door and let us both in. "Babe, is that you?" Leyanna called from the kitchen.

"Yeah. I brought my aunt with me," I called back to her.

I heard the sink go off and her slippers slide across the floor.

When she appeared in the living room, she had one of my long T-shirts on with a pair of slippers.

"Benji, you should have warned me. I look a hot mess. Hey, how are you?" She smiled and went to shake my aunt's hand.

"Girl, we both look a mess, but he insisted I had to come over right away. A handshake? We do hugs around here." She laughed and pulled Leyanna into a hug.

"Y'all hungry? I made some turkey loaf with mashed potatoes and corn."

"Damn, yeah, I'm type hungry. I'll be back. Y'all start," I told her and went upstairs. Taking my watch and shit off, I changed into basketball shorts and a tank top. I went to my rug that I had in the corner in the bedroom and sat down to say a quick prayer for Lilly.

Once I was finished, I joined Leyanna and my aunt downstairs. They were talking and laughing like they had known each other their entire lives. Leyanna was listening to my aunt's crazy ass life she lived. Hopefully, that baby would calm her the hell down.

"Your aunt is hilarious. You coming back for the wedding, right?"

"Sweet pea, I ain't leaving. Chy said I can stay at her place because she's never there."

"She's been there more lately since her and her man been going through it. Where is she anyway?"

"Probably with her fiancé and the baby. She told me to make myself at home and left. I'm supposed to go over there tomorrow."

"Cool. Has she showed you our boutique yet?"

"Y'all got a boutique? Chy didn't mention that to me." She gasped. Chyna probably didn't mention it because her head wasn't into it anymore.

"I have to show it to you sometime this week, if you want to see it," Leyanna suggested.

"Of course. Might can find me some cute clothes since that closet in my room is pretty big."

"Cool. Come eat, baby." She placed my plate in front of me at the head of the table. She bent down and kissed me on the forehead before going to get hers. We chilled and ate while Leyanna filled her in on the plans she had for our wedding.

20

SOLACE

"AALIYAH, WHERE THE FUCK YOU AT?" I called as I walked into the house. I had been calling her phone all morning, and she hadn't answered. I was at another chick's house last night and decided to let Aaliyah chill out.

"I'm in the kitchen," she called out.

When I got to the kitchen, she was sitting at the table with a bowl of cereal. She had on some short ass boy shorts that made my dick hard. Aaliyah smiled when she saw me. I stayed out last night, and she didn't call me or nag me like Lilly would do. Instead, she stayed her ass in the crib and worried about getting her head in the books.

"What you did last night?" I sat down and looked at her.

She abandoned her bowl and went to pull eggs and bacon out the fridge. I didn't even need to say shit about me being hungry. Aaliyah just knew what to do without me having to tell her. That was why she was up in this crib and didn't have to worry about paying the bills.

"I studied and watched TV. How was your night?"

"Same shit. I was thinking we should go out to the mall, get you some clothes and shit," I offered.

My ear had been to the street, and it seemed like Lilly's baby father wasn't looking for me. Kash's bum ass would always be looking for me, but I wasn't worried about him and what he could possibly do. He had Tike handling all his business and making sure BMS was straight.

"Really? I'm excited to spend some time with you, babe." She smiled as she cracked eggs into the bowl.

"I'm about to go lay down. Bring my food when you're done," I told her, and she walked over to kiss me on the lips.

I went into the bedroom and laid out on the bed. The night before, I was at my freak's house, and she wore my ass out. After snorting coke off her pussy, we were pretty much done for the night. The fact that I didn't have to worry about explaining where I'd been to Aaliyah made me feel that much better. She was just happy to see me this morning, nothing else. I didn't have to make false promises about not cheating on her. She was happy just being provided this crib and occasionally going to the mall so she could get what she wanted.

"Here, babe," she said and handed me a plate with waffles, eggs, and bacon. I sat up and slapped her on the ass.

"Thank you, ma. Come suck this dick while I eat," I told her, and she did as she was told. My jeans were being pulled down, and my dick was being released. She took that shit in her mouth while I ate and watched SportsCenter. Nobody couldn't tell me that this wasn't heaven on earth.

"You like that?" she asked when she popped it out of her mouth. I laughed and took my hand, then slapped her in the mouth with my dick.

"Keep sucking until I nut in your mouth," I ordered, and she obliged to what I was asking. "Shit feel like everything," I moaned and finished my food.

I was full as fuck with a hard dick. I lay back and let Aaliyah do her thing until I was cumming in her mouth. She had sucked until I was empty and then left the room to brush her teeth. I was laid out and ready to catch some sleep before going to the mall with her.

$$$

"WE GOT SO MUCH STUFF." Aaliyah was so excited with all the shit I bought her. She acted like I took her to Saks and shit. All she got was a few outfits, some heels, and sneakers. The smallest shit made her happy, so I didn't have to spend bread like I spent with Lilly's expensive ass.

I held her hand, and we walked around the mall and continued to pick up random shit she wanted. She was really showing out by kissing and hugging on me. It was as if she wanted everyone to know that she was my girl. All my other chicks knew I had different chicks, and as long as I broke them off with money for their hair and nails, they didn't care. Aaliyah stopped short in her steps and was looking.

"Leyanna?" she called out.

The two women turned around and looked at her. That was when I realized that one of the chicks was Kash's girl. It was obvious that the tall ass nigga behind her was a bodyguard. He wasn't fooling nobody trying to act all casual with his big ass.

"Aaliyah? Hey," the other chick said dryly.

Aaliyah walked up to them and was talking. I stayed back just in case shorty knew who I was. I was sitting on the bench for fifteen minutes before she walked back over to me. Little did her ass know, I had a plan for her ass.

"I'm ready, babe," she said and grabbed my hand to pull me up. "I'm going to cook us something good tonight."

"Oh, word? Who was that?" I asked as we walked to the parking lot.

"My old roommate and her friend. We fell out over some foolishness, and now it looks like we might be able to reconnect. We could probably double date with their men," she suggested. Unless she wanted me dead, that was a dumb ass move, and I would continue to curve her each time she asked.

We placed the bags in the car and got in before heading back to the house. As we drove, I thought to myself how this just fell in my lap. Shit was like gold sitting right on my lap, and I couldn't touch it until Aaliyah told me to.

"Do you think I can get a car? Nothing expensive, just to get around. I hate taking cabs and being trapped in the house," she asked sweetly.

On one hand, I didn't need her ass getting a car because she would think it was cool to pop up on me. Then again, I needed her to come through for me. I didn't know if I should put her up on game or let her get in there first then tell her.

"I think that's cool. We can go look soon. You need to hang with your friends more too," I threw out there.

"I don't have friends, Solace."

"Those girls in the mall; start hanging back with them."

She sighed. "I can try. I do need some more friends."

"Yeah, you do." That was all I needed to hear to formulate my plan for Kash's girl.

21

LEYANNA

"WELL, THAT WAS INTERESTING," Chyna said as we sat down for lunch.

"Aaliyah, right? I'm not paying that girl any mind." I waved the situation off like it didn't just happen.

"Ley, she gave you her number to make things right... just reach out to her," Chyna suggested.

I stopped fucking with Aaliyah because she was fake. She talked shit about me and was the reason I had to move in with Chyna. We didn't see each other much on the campus because I was barely in class and did online classes mostly. The only time I came in was to speak to my academic advisors, then I was gone.

"Maybe I shouldn't be so mean," I said and looked over the menu. "Anyway, it was nice to get out with you." I laughed.

"Girl, I'm so glad that Kash took the baby and is spending the day with him. I needed to get some clothes for the fall." She giggled.

"Benji wants to get married this month. I'm thinking about doing something small."

"Have it in Kash's backyard. It's nice out there. We can get some flowers and stuff and bam. Just need a dress now," she offered.

"I'll run it by Benji," I said.

The waiter took our order, and we sipped our drinks while talking about her and Kash's relationship. Quite frankly, I was tired of hearing about their issues. Here I was trying to plan a wedding for me and Benji, and she was complaining about Kash staying out an hour late. Benji was about to go to New York for a few months, and she was worried about Kash staying out an hour late. I rummaged through my bag for my ringing cell phone before I located it.

"Hey, Khloe," I greeted.

"Umm, so are we going to get hours this week? I know you said you went away, but I have bills to pay," she started. Damn, I couldn't even get a hey or anything. Since being back, I told the girls that the store would be closed for the week. I had work to catch up on for school, and I knew Chyna needed a little break from opening the store when I was gone.

"The store was just closed for the week. I'll be back open this weekend," I informed her.

"Uhh, the store has been closed since you left for your birthday."

I looked at Chyna, and she seemed unbothered, going through her phone. "Let me call you right back."

"I've been trying to get these sneakers for Baby Kash and can't." She sulked.

"It seems like all you care about is Baby Kash and big Kash lately," I said just as the waiter slid our plates onto the table.

"What? That's my kid and fiancé. Of course I care about them."

"I've been busting my ass to finish school and run our store while I let you be a mother and fiancée to big Kash and lil Kash. I asked you to open and close the store for a week, and you couldn't even do that; all I asked of you and your *so busy* life. You wanted to open the shop and haven't done shit for it!" I yelled.

"Leyanna, it's not that serious. I have a baby, school, and a man to try to take care of. I closed the week as a vacation for all of us... Why are you complaining?"

"Are you serious? I can't even deal with you right now." I grabbed my purse and scooted out the booth.

"Leyanna, come back," she called behind me, but I was already on my way out the door. As I exited the restaurant, I used my app to get a cab so I could head home. It was ridiculous that she didn't think that this was fucked up on her part. Our store couldn't afford to miss out on money, yet she allowed that to happen.

I was so mad that I had to get up before I said something she didn't like. It pissed me off that the store wasn't a concern for her. The store was my entire life right now, and she couldn't care less about it. The cab pulled up, and I jumped inside just as she was coming out the restaurant. Right now, I had nothing to say to her because it pissed me off even thinking about the situation. Ugh, why couldn't she be as motivated as I was about our store? When we talked about opening it, she was so excited like me. Now she acted as if it was a hassle in her life.

I got out of the cab and went into the house. Benji was sitting on the couch with a bottle of water. He must have finished working out because he was all sweaty. I flung myself right into his arms and cried from frustration.

"What happened, Wiz?"

"Your sister couldn't come through for me and had the store closed when we were in Paris... She acts like it wasn't a big deal. Ughhhhhhhh!" I screamed out into his chest.

"Where she at now?"

"I left her at the mall. Why couldn't she just do that one

thing? I understand Kash has money and she's set, but come on. Doesn't she want something for herself?" I vented.

"You set too. Fuck you talking about?" Benji got all defensive like I knew he would.

"Yeah, but this is more than you doing for me, babe. I want to do this so I can be proud of myself."

"I hear you..." He allowed his voice to trail off.

"I'm so upset; why would she do that? You honestly need to talk to her." I sucked my teeth and got off the couch. "You ate yet?"

Benji shook his head no. "You?"

"I left in the middle of us eating. If I stayed there any longer, I would have had some choice words for her. Babe, you wanna have Sunday dinner at my dad's tomorrow? You know, let him know about all of this," I hinted.

He turned and looked at me. "I've been ready; your dad knows this?"

"I'm going to call him and ask him if we can come over. I just want y'all to have a relationship if you're going to be my husband."

"Alright. I'm down with whatever will make you happy."

I kissed him on the lips and went upstairs to call my father. After listening to the phone ring for what seemed like ten minutes, my dad's voice came on the line. I felt bad because I didn't go around or answer his calls as much as I should.

"Hey, baby girl!" he greeted me.

"Hey, Daddy! What are you doing?"

"A little of this and that; your brother has me running crazy for his school supplies." He laughed.

"I miss you guys. Are you having Sunday dinner?"

"You know it; your mama went to get some onions, peppers, and other stuff," he told me.

I wanted to break down and cry because I had pushed my

family to the side. Between school and everything else, I'd neglected spending time with my little brother and parents. My mother had been back living with my father, and I hadn't checked in on them.

"I'm so sorry, Daddy," I said, sniffling into the phone

"For what, Leyanna? Is everything good with you?" He grew concerned.

"Not coming around like I should have. I have so much to catch you guys up on. I'm getting married," I revealed. In a way, I felt like he should know before we came to dinner.

"You're getting what?"

"Married. He treats me well and wants me to be his wife."

"Who, Benji?"

"Yes, I'm gonna bring him tomorrow; is that alright?"

My father chuckled in the phone. "If he's going to be your husband, then we need to have a chat, so yes, bring him."

"I'll see you guys tomorrow, and remember, don't cook pork. He's Muslim."

"Leyanna, that's a conversation that we need to have... You know what being Muslim entails?"

"He's Muslim, not me, Daddy."

"Ley, you don't think he'll want you to convert? What about when you have kids?" He sighed before speaking again. "I want to speak to him and see where his head is at with all of this."

"Alright. See y'all tomorrow," I told him, and we ended the call.

I lay back on the bed and thought about what my father said. Would Benji expect me to convert? So caught up in the hype of being his wife, I didn't take all of that into consideration. How would we raise our children? There was a lot to consider, and for some strange reason, it didn't scare me. I was still ready to marry this man and love him with all of my heart. My father had met Benji, and they didn't really have that much of a conversation, especially since my father didn't think we would be together for much longer. He knew my track record with men and wasn't falling for the hype until I'd actually been with someone for a little while.

"Ley, can you make something to eat?" Benji called from downstairs. "Please, Wiz," he added.

"Coming, babe," I said and went to fix my big baby something to eat. I needed some time to deal with Chyna and the mess with the store. Did I even want to have the store anymore? Her lack of motivation was making me question everything.

$$$

"YOU TOLD him I don't eat pork, right? I'm not trying to have that shit pushed in my face," Benji said as he leaned back in the passenger's seat.

We pulled into my father's driveway, and I killed the engine. All night, I tossed and turned thinking about today. It was as if Benji was meeting my father for the first time all over again. I just didn't want my father to start with all his questions I was sure he had. All I wanted was Benji and my father to form a bond, an amazing relationship. In the past, I had been neglecting my family, and after yesterday, I promised myself that I wouldn't do that anymore.

"Babe, I told them already... You nervous?"

"No," he said and came around to open the driver's side door for me. "I met your father before."

Stepping out, I grabbed his hand and kissed him on the lips. We walked up the stairs. The screen door was open, so I opened it and pulled Benji behind me.

"Hey, Zack!" I yelled when I saw my brother walking down

the stairs. He looked at me and smiled as I rushed into his arms. "I swear you are growing a foot a day," I joked.

"Dang, Ley, where you been?"

Sighing, I hugged him tighter. "Here, there, and everywhere," I joked.

"Hey, Benji." Zack nodded at Benji, and he returned the same gesture. "Mama is upstairs sleeping; she came in late last night."

I shook my head because my mother hadn't changed one bit. "Where's Daddy?"

"In the kitchen cooking... He been in there since this morning. Tell him I'll be back for dinner," Zack called out just as a car was pulling up.

"Where you going?"

"To my girl's house." He smirked and left out the door. Dang, my little brother had a girlfriend, and I hadn't even known.

I walked to the kitchen with Benji, and my father was stirring something in the pot. It had the whole house smelling so good. "Daddy!"

"Leyanna," he said and hugged me. "You need to start coming around more often."

"I know, Daddy." Benji extended his hand and shook my father's hand.

"How are you doing, sir?"

"Man, just call me Zeek," he said.

"No problem," Benji said and stepped back.

"I cooked your favorite, baby girl."

My greedy ass went and looked in the pot, and there was my favorite: gumbo.

"Yesss, I can't wait to get a bowl. I hope you made extra, because I'm gonna need to bring some home." I did a little dance.

"Come on in the living room. I'm waiting for those greens to simmer more. I heard you're not big on pork, so I put the pork ribs up for tomorrow night."

"I appreciate it," Benji said and held onto my waist as we walked into the living room. Me and Benji sat down on the loveseat and my father sat in his recliner.

"So Benji, last time we saw each other, you didn't tell me much about yourself," my father said.

Benji pulled me tighter to him and spoke. "I own a sneaker store in New York, raised my little sister, who is in college, and love Allah."

My father looked at him and nodded his head. "Your parents?"

"My mother was murdered when I was sixteen."

"I'm sorry to hear about that."

"It's fine."

"Ley tells me that you're a Muslim... You expect Leyanna to convert? We're Christians," my father just had to bring up.

"Daddy!"

"Ley, you wanna marry him, and that's your right. However, I need to know what you're about to get into." He held his hand up and looked at Benji with a serious expression. Benji leaned up and matched his.

"At some point, I would hope she would want to. If she doesn't, it doesn't make me love her any less."

"What about if you decide to have kids? They won't celebrate Christmas, Easter, and shit like that?" my father continued with the poking.

"Daddy, he celebrates Christmas for me... and if we have kids, I'm sure he'll do the same."

"What about the kids being christened? How you feel about that?"

Benji put his hands together and looked my father right in the eyes. "When we get there, then we'll discuss it. I'm not closed-minded and will consider her feelings with anything she's feeling."

"Understandable," my father said and nodded his head.

"Ley! When did you get here?" My mother wiped the sleep out of her eyes. I got up and hugged her before returning back to my seat.

"I came over for Sunday dinner," I told her.

"How you doing, Benji?" she greeted and sat down on the arm of my father's chair. "Where's Zack? With that girl?"

"Yeah, when did that happen? Y'all let him have a girl-friend?" I joked.

"He's a teenager and is old enough. Soon as those grades start slipping, then him and his little relationship is over."

"That's reasonable. I doubt he'll do that."

"Benji, how did you keep your sister on course? She's in college with Ley, right?"

"Yeah. I just rewarded her for good grades," he answered.

"How is she?"

"She's fine."

I knew he didn't like to talk about Chyna because he felt like he failed with her. School wasn't a priority to Chyna like a bunch of other things. When it came to Kash, she made sure to drop whatever and tend to him and their child. It pissed Benji off, and he couldn't say anything.

"Y'all ready to eat?"

"Yessss!" I jumped up. We continued to talk while we sat around and ate some of the food my father prepared. It felt good being around my family. My mother even seemed like she was doing so much better. I had to make sure I made a healthy balance between work, school, Benji, and my family.

22

KASH

"WHAT YOU DOING, PRINCESS?" I asked as she sat in my office with a notepad and a phone stuck to her ear.

She sighed and looked at me with bags under her eyes. It didn't look like she slept at all since I left around two this morning. I had to head out to meet with Tike. While my frustration was boiling over with the disappearance of Solace, I couldn't help but to feel good when it came to BMS. We were making more moves and money in the same breath. Everyone wanted to get down with us and couldn't. The money was piling in, and all I could do was put it up for Chyna and the baby. If something were to happen to me, I wanted to make sure they and my parents were taken care of.

"Your son is fussy and wouldn't go down to bed until an hour after you left. Then, I couldn't sleep because of the fight me and Leyanna had. So I'm gonna plan her wedding; she can't stay mad at me if I do that."

"About the store? Y'all still not talking?"

"Nope, and I want to come to her with all my ducks in the

row. She really cares about the store, and I do too, but it's too much to handle sometimes." She sighed in frustration.

"You and Ley are friends, and if this wedding goes through, she'll be your sister-in-law. You definitely need to make things right."

"I'm trying," she replied and picked up her ringing cell phone.

She seemed to be so busy, so I left her alone and went to spend time with my son. My mother had gone home and came up every other weekend to visit with her grandbaby. You couldn't tell her that Baby Kash wasn't hers. She loved him, and it showed from the way she made the effort to take time away from her life to help me and Chyna out with him. Chyna was still learning about being a mother and juggling college.

When I walked into my son's room, he was sleeping peacefully. I bent down and kissed him on his forehead, then sat in the chair in his room. Since almost losing my life, family meant everything to me. I wanted to marry Chyna in the future and have more children with her. Still, I was hiding the secret of killing her mother. Benji agreed to keep the secret because he wanted his sister to be happy. It didn't mean that he was going to make things easier for me. Whenever I was around him, he was cordial and spoke, yet I could see it in his eyes. It was killing him to keep this away from his sister.

"Sooo, guess who just planned their wedding? Well, not all the way, but almost." Chyna clapped her hands but stopped when she realized that our son was still peacefully sleeping.

"Oh yeah?" I reached for her to sit on my lap.

Kissing her on the neck, I allowed her to tell me her plans. "So, it's going to be on a nice private beach in Tampa. Right before the sunset, and they'll be going on their honeymoon straight from the wedding. Benji didn't want a reception, which is weird, but not for Benji. I just thought that Leyanna would want one, but whatever Benji wants, she wants." She rambled on about her brother's upcoming nuptials.

"Give them what they want. When you gonna talk to her?"

She leaned back on my shoulder and looked into the crib beside us. "I'm trying to give her some space."

"Don't you think she should be looking for a dress or all that shit y'all do to get ready for a wedding?"

"Uh, so you think when we get married, it'll be shit, Kairo?" She turned and looked at me.

"No. You know what I mean, Princess."

"I guess I should go to the shop this week and talk to her. I've been neglecting the shop, and I can't help but feel like my mind isn't in it."

"Then you need to tell her so y'alls friendship won't be affected by it. Princess, she asked you a favor, and you let her and your employees down. You want our son to be like that? Make the shit right with her because you're the one that's to blame."

"Ugh, why do you have to be so right?" She laughed and got off my lap. "I need to find someone to officiate the wedding. Then Benji wants it to be on a Sunday because it starts a fresh week."

"You can do it, babe; make that shit right," I said, and she stormed off to finish planning her brother's wedding. I laid back in the chair and took a nap with my son sitting beside me.

23

CHYNA

THE CLASS WAS DISMISSED, and I rushed out the class-room and straight to the parking lot. I had just taken a test and was sure I aced it. After speaking to Benji about everything, he was cool with all that I had planned. The only person I had to speak to about everything was Leyanna. The wedding was less than two weeks away, and the only person that had any clue of it was Benji. I was on my way to the boutique now to tell Leyanna about it.

"Chyna!" I heard and stopped speed walking through the halls and turned around. It was Aaliyah jogging toward me with a smile on her face.

"Hey, Aaliyah!" I smiled and decided to be nice. She did voice how she was wrong and that she was trying to change.

"I saw you coming out of class and decided to see how you were doing," she said as she placed her bag on her right arm.

I smiled and looked down at my Rolex. Time was of the essence, and I needed to make it to the boutique before Leyanna left. "I'm good, just heading to the boutique."

"Oh yeah, I need to come there to get some clothes. I heard you guys have some dope clothes."

"So I've been told." I laughed.

"I know you guys probably think I'm fake as hell. I didn't do any better by behaving that way. I'm just trying to finish school and find positive people to hang with. I respect y'all and would like a second chance."

How could I tell her that she couldn't hang with us? Everyone deserved a second chance, and Aaliyah seemed to be changing or had changed. "We can have lunch tomorrow after class. You down?"

"Sure, here's my number," she said and handed me a card with a number and email on it. "I'm trying to make some cash by doing bookkeeping for businesses."

I didn't know if I would trust her going over my books, but I was glad she had a little side business going for herself.

"Cool. I'll give you a call tomorrow to see if you can still come."

"Cool. Tell Leyanna I said hey."

"Sure."

I rushed to my car, started it, and then pulled out my parking spot to head to the boutique. It was nice that Aaliyah wanted to speak and have a nice conversation, but I was a mother, college student, and businesswoman that was doubling as a damn wedding planner. Benji had spent so much of his life making sure that I was fine and doing well that this was something I could do for both him and Leyanna. It took me no time to get to the boutique and pull into the parking lot. I killed the engine and walked into the store. Leyanna was sitting in the front on her laptop.

"Hey," she dryly greeted me.

The two employees were helping customers and hanging up the new inventory. The store was beautiful and was all Leyanna's vision. I never had a particular vision for the store, and since I was pregnant, I didn't help at all with it. It looked so nice, and everything was in place. It even smelled like strawberries when you walked through the glass doors.

"Hey, can we talk in the office?" I asked her, and she nodded.

"Khloe, take over the front for me, please?"

"Sure, Leyanna," she said and replaced Leyanna behind the desk. We went to the office and closed the door behind us.

Leyanna sat down behind her desk, and I looked at mine. How did I miss this? She had got us both desks for the office that were identical. Not really; Leyanna's desk had more scattered papers and things all over it. I walked over and sat down behind mine.

"I miss you, Ley," I started.

She didn't look moved at all. "Oh, you had time to actually miss me with your busy life?"

"I know I've been messing up, and I'm sorry. I should have opened the store and did what you asked of me. I'm just not into this as much as you are."

"I understand that completely. You should have told me this wasn't for you. Instead, you let me believe this is what you wanted."

"I'm sorry. My mind just has been all over, and I can't focus. With school and the baby, it's all too much. I've been trying to keep up with the store, but I'm not you. Which leaves me to one of my many surprises."

She laughed and looked at me. "Chy, I don't need surprises right now. I need to plan a wedding and run this business."

"Shhhh, let me finish," I interrupted her.

"I want you to have my half of the shop. You made this vision possible, and I shouldn't reap the benefits of all the hard work you've put in for this."

"Chy, noooo," she tried to object, but I put my hand up.

"Yes. This is your vision, and that's all I'm going to say about that. Keep my desk because I'll need somewhere to come and get away from the baby and Kash."

"Never." She smiled as she wiped the tears that slid down her face.

"Next, we need to find you a wedding dress and get you fitted. Your wedding is in two weeks, and it'll be in Tampa on a beach. Everything is basically taken care of since y'all aren't having a reception. I wish y'all would have one, though."

"I just wanna go on our honeymoon because Benji goes to the city a few days after the date you're telling me."

"About your honeymoon. I've arranged for you both to have a penthouse suite in New York to enjoy the city. Of course, after, you'll fly back, and Benji will be in New York."

"Wow. You did all this for me or because you fucked up?" she joked.

"A little of both, but I want you and Benji to be happy. It took a little out my schedule, but I managed to almost complete it, and I'm excited for y'all."

"I appreciate that, Chyna. It means the world that you decided to plan this for us. I know Benji will be happy."

"Girl, he already knows." I laughed.

"Y'all think y'all slick." She laughed. "I guess I should be trying to find a wedding gown now."

"Yep. Oh, I ran into Aaliyah and invited her to lunch. You should come along and invite her to the wedding."

"I don't know about all of that."

"Come on. She seems genuine and even has her own little business doing bookkeeping for small companies."

"That's nice for her," she said.

"Yeah, so be open and be nice to her... because you're coming."

"Fine," she finally agreed and looked over some papers. "Want to go shopping for some dresses?"

"Hell yeah! Come on." I jumped up and grabbed my bags.

She laughed, and we headed to go shopping for her dress. I couldn't wait to see her in a beautiful dress, and to pick myself one out too.

24

BENJI

I RUSHED through the doors of the hospital and laid my eyes on JoJo, who was sitting by Lilly's bedside. His eyes were red, and tears were sliding down his cheeks. Soon as I got the call from Renee, I dropped everything and made sure I made it here. Lilly had passed during the night. A blood clot had gone to her lung, and she passed in her sleep. When JoJo came by in the morning, they told him to take all the time he needed before they moved her body to the morgue, yet they didn't expect him to be in her room for twelve hours. It was now eight at night, and he hadn't moved from her side. Renee called me an hour ago after she came to bring him some lunch. My heart hurt for Jolie and Lilly's mother.

"JoJo, you gotta let them take her," I said and placed my hand on his back. He looked up at me with so much hurt in his eyes.

He and Lilly's relationship wasn't perfect, but somehow, they made it work for them. He stepped up in his role as Jolie's father, and their problems seemed to have faded away. How was he going to explain to his daughter that her mother was gone? He had told me that she was asking for her mother and wanted to see her. Now, how was he supposed to explain that she'd never see her mother again?

"They can't take her because she's going to wake up again, Benji. She gotta wake up for Jolie. I can't raise her on my own, man," he stressed as he looked into my eyes. All I could see through the red was pain.

"This shit ain't easy, Jo. Lilly wouldn't have had a baby with you if she didn't think you were capable of raising her. It's going to be hard, but you and Renee got this."

"How the fuck am I going to do this, Benji? Please tell me how the fuck I'm gonna do this shit!" he barked and threw the chair against the door.

I stood in the corner and stepped back. There was nothing I could do to make this situation better. He had to know that Jolie would always be good. It was bad that she didn't have her mother and fucked up because of what happened to her, but he still had to raise her. He had to raise Jolie; he was all she had.

"You can do this shit, bro. I'm right here along with Mookie. We'll help you with Jolie and help you get through this shit. You hear me!" I walked over and grabbed his arms.

He had tears sliding down his face as he tried to get out of my embrace. "Why would that nigga do this shit to her? The cops keep lurking around and asking if I know where the fuck that nigga is. Why the fuck would I know!" he continued to scream.

I pulled him out the room so the doctors and nurses could get her out the room. He had been in there too long with her dead body. After a while, he stopped fighting and got himself together.

"I need to tell her moms," he mumbled and walked down the hall. I followed behind him as we went to the elevator and rode to her floor. As we stepped off the elevator and walked to her room, I felt like we were the Grim Reaper, like we were about to take someone's life.

I allowed JoJo to go in there alone. He knew Lilly's mother

more than I did. He should be the one to break this news to her. It didn't take long before I heard someone screaming at the top of their lungs. JoJo didn't beat around the bush, so I knew he went in there and told it to her straight. The nurses rushed from the station and into the room. Lilly's mother was screaming from the top of her lungs for about ten minutes. After the first few minutes, I thought she would get tired and stop. She finally quieted down, and I continued to sit and wait for JoJo to leave out the room.

"Such a shame. Woman lost her daughter and doesn't have any family," the nurse said to the doctor as they exited the room.

"God won't give us more than we can handle, Sherald," he replied as they walked down the hall after tossing their used gloves into the wastebasket.

JoJo came out the room with his head down and walked to the elevator. Sometimes, the best thing you could do for someone was to allow them silence. Don't tell them a bunch of shit like they'll be good and they'll pull through. Let them sit in their silence and process everything. That's exactly what I was going to do. We walked through the parking lot and JoJo stopped.

"I'm gonna catch up with you when I get my head cleared. Trust that I'm good to get home." He looked me in the eyes.

"Hit me when you get to the crib. You know me and Mookie here for you, bruh," I said and hugged him.

"I know. I just need to be with Jolie and Renee right now."

We embraced in a brotherly hug before we parted ways. I wasn't about to rest without knowing he got home, so I followed him. Once he made it to his crib, I watched him walk inside with his head down and hands in his pocket. It fucked me up knowing I couldn't do anything to help him. I headed back home to go pray for Lilly and her family.

When I walked into the crib, Leyanna ducked behind the couch and peeked her head over to look at me. "What the fuck, babe?" I questioned and tried to walk behind the couch, but she screamed.

"Benji! This is my dress, and you can't see!" she warned.

"Why the hell you standing in the middle of the living room with it then?" I questioned and walked upstairs, trying to resist the urge to see the dress.

I caught the tail end of her running into the spare bedroom on the ground floor. I laughed because when she came out, she had on panties and a bra. Leyanna had this whole vision of refraining from sex until after we were married. It was hard to resist her when she was standing in front of me damn near naked.

"How is JoJo?" she questioned. I didn't make it fully upstairs, so I sat on the step. Leyanna came and climbed into my lap.

"She's gone, and he ain't taking that shit well." I sighed.

She touched my face and kissed me on the lips. "I'm sorry, baby."

"I don't know what he's doing about a funeral right now... I'm gonna give him time with the baby and getting his mind right before asking him."

"If we have to, we can push the wedding back."

I shook my head. "He wouldn't want me to do that."

"You sure?" She caressed my face and looked at me.

"Yeah. I know my brother."

"Okay. I'm excited to be your wife, Benji." She smiled and looked me into my eyes.

"I can't wait until you're Mrs. Benji Johnson." I rubbed her ass.

She kissed me on the lips before she went to go do whatever the hell she was doing before I walked into the door. I went upstairs and went to pray for Jolie and JoJo. You could never have too many prayers, and they needed all the ones they could get right about now.

$$$

RENEE LET me in the apartment the next morning. I couldn't go on about my day knowing I hadn't come by and checked on him. When I walked into the crib, JoJo was sitting on the couch, looking into space. The TV wasn't on, and he didn't even know that I was in the crib.

"How's the baby?" I asked Renee, and she pulled me in the kitchen.

She started wiping down the already clean counter. I guess that was her way of coping with everything going on.

"He's been quiet since he came in last night. He put Jolie in the bed, and they slept all night. This morning, neither of them are making noise, talking, or anything. I'm afraid to tell him that I'm pregnant," she revealed to me.

I hadn't even been in the crib for fifteen minutes, and the silence was killing me. You could literally hear the clock ticking, which would irritate the shit out of me.

"Where's Jolie?" I looked around.

"I just put her down for a nap. She sits around and doesn't laugh or anything. I think she knows something, Benji," she whined.

"Lilly and him had a bond beyond having Jolie. They were friends before anything, so this shit is hurting him badly."

"I totally understand that. Yet, I don't know if we're going to make your wedding, and I feel so bad."

I touched Renee's shoulder because she was bugging out. "We'll have a bigger wedding in the future. It ain't a big deal." I tried to comfort her.

After making sure she was straight, I went and sat down next to JoJo. He looked at me and nodded then returned to staring into space.

"How did you sleep last night?"

"Regular."

"You can't shut Renee out. She's worried, and you're going to stress her and the baby out," I slipped and mentioned.

It didn't matter if she was keeping it a secret or not. Stressing wasn't good for her or their unborn baby. JoJo needed to come together with Renee and Jolie because they were his family. Shutting Renee out because she didn't feel the same amount of hurt that he felt wasn't right. Renee was hurting for Jolie, and that counted for something. Jolie would never have that relationship with her mother that other girls had. Renee could step in and do what Lilly was, yet it wasn't the same. Losing my mother young wasn't a walk in the park, so I knew JoJo had a lot to go through once she fully understood things.

"She's pregnant?"

"Yeah. She's been wanting to tell you, and then this happened."

"Damn."

"Stop letting her stress out, because she's worried. She in there cleaning clean counters." I tried to lighten the mood, and JoJo laughed.

"I feel you; this shit just a hard pill to swallow. Lilly was just straight, and then this happens. Her moms is going crazy; the hospital been calling all morning. This shit is fucked up, and I want that nigga dead."

"It's as good as done. I'll keep my ear to the streets and see where that nigga hiding at."

"Bet."

I stayed for a little bit then headed back to the crib. Knowing JoJo was going try to put one foot in front of the next made me feel accomplished. He was about to be a father for the second time, so he needed to make things right with Renee so she could have a healthy pregnancy.

25

LEYANNA

IT WAS crazy how wherever Chyna was, Aaliyah was there too. It was bad enough that she brought this girl to my dress fitting after I told her not to. I couldn't understand why Chyna was so hell bent on making a friendship work with this girl. She was the one who told me about her shady ass, and now she wanted to bring her around like we were all best friends. I didn't have any present issue with Aaliyah, so I tolerated her being around. She did seem genuine, yet I wasn't willing to take that chance with her ass right about now. Currently, there was too much on my plate for me. With the wedding a few days away, Benji worried about JoJo, and having to think of my future husband being in another state for the first few months of our marriage, it was too much for me to deal with.

"What you thinking about, Wiz?" Benji questioned as he climbed into the bed with me. I had a cool washcloth over my head as I tried to relax for a few.

"Do you want to get married now, or should we wait until you're finished with the job?"

He pulled me closer to him and looked into my eyes. "I wanna marry you. Stop asking and second-guessing shit."

"Benji, I think I'm pregnant!" I blurted.

It had been all I could think about the past two weeks I had missed my period. I had bought pregnancy tests and been too afraid to use them. Then, a part of me wanted to know what it would feel like to be someone's mother. Chyna couldn't sit still for more than five minutes, yet when she had Baby Kash, it seemed like her world was perfect, and she had all the time in the world. Benji held my chin and forced me to look into his face.

"You serious, or you fucking with me?"

I sat up and ran my hand through my hair. "I really don't know because I haven't got my period, and my breasts have been so sore. I googled, and those are symptoms."

"You need me to run and get a test?" He started trying to slip off the bed. I could tell he was all too excited to hear that he might have gotten me knocked up.

"I have some in my purse," I told him. "Downstairs."

Benji didn't bother to let me get the rest of my sentence out before he was zipping down the stairs and coming back with the box I bought. He opened it up and handed me the contents inside of the box.

"Want me to come in with you?" he eagerly asked.

I turned to him and laughed. "I think I have it from here. I'll call you when I'm done."

Opening the package, I read the instructions and took a deep breath. This little piece of plastic could change my life in five minutes. As soon as the words popped up on the screen, it could be changed forever. Sticking the stick between my legs, I allowed the urine to sprinkle on the tip of the pregnancy test. When I was finished, I wiped myself, capped the test, and called Benji into the bathroom. We stood in the middle of the bathroom holding each other because we didn't know what to expect. After what seemed like an eternity, Benji picked up the test.

"You're not pregnant," he revealed, and I sighed a breath of relief on the low. On the other hand, Benji looked disappointed as he tossed the test into the bathroom trash, and then went to lay on the bed.

"Babe, it'll happen soon, I promise," I told him and kissed him on the lips. He wasn't too upset to kiss me back.

At first, I wanted nothing to do with having a child. Then, when I thought about how Benji was so excited and wanted children more than anything, I couldn't see myself not giving him children. He was a good man and didn't ask for much, so why couldn't I give him a child? I could still run my business and go to school along with having the baby. God knew the timing was off, which was why he made that a negative test.

"I hear you." He sighed and closed his eyes. I laid down on his chest because this would the small peace and quiet before the wedding.

$$$

My wedding day was finally here, and I was so excited. My mother was in the car with me as we drove to Tampa for the wedding. Today, I was going to become Benji's wife, something I had fought him on. Here I was, about to be his rib, the right to his wrong, and his one and only. Nerves had set in the night before when I couldn't sleep. I tossed and turned all night, thinking of today, and now it was finally here. My father and brother were in a car with Benji. We didn't want something big and dramatic; just close friends and family was fine with us.

"You excited for this big step?"

I smiled as I looked at my mother and nodded my head. "I can't believe that you're getting married." She smiled and hugged me. "We've had our differences, but you know I'm trying to be there for Zack and now you," she offered a side smile.

"Just keep trying," was all I could say.

The fact that she was even here to witness me getting married was a big step on her part. All I wanted was positivity around me for this day. Anything that she did in the past was the past, and I was looking forward to the future with my husband. It was funny how I didn't want marriage and kids, but now I was thinking about the day we would welcome a baby into the world. The failed pregnancy test made me sigh a breath of relief, but looking at how disappointed Benji was made me hurt for him. He wanted kids and the whole nine, and he did deserve it. I still had worries with his choice of career.

"We're here," my mother said as the car pulled into the circular driveway of the resort. Chyna was waiting there with Aaliyah. I opened the door, and Chyna hugged me tightly.

"We'll be sisters after today!" She squealed.

I hugged her back even tighter and laughed. "We're already like sisters, but this will make it official. Hey, Aaliyah." I smiled and hugged her as well.

"Congratulations, Leyanna." She hugged me back.

Chyna grabbed me and my mother's hands and pulled us inside the resort. She had a room waiting for me to get my makeup and hair done and to put my dress on. Inside the suite, there were fresh fruit, champagne, and some food.

"Since you didn't want a reception, I had a caterer make us some different foods to eat while we're getting ready."

I turned to her and gave her hug. "This is so nice, Chy." I hugged her again, and we laughed to keep from crying.

"It's the least I could do for you, Ley. You make Benji so happy, and I haven't seen him open up to someone in a long time. Plus, we didn't get to have a bridal shower or bachelorette party."

She sat me down in the makeup chair as she and Aaliyah put

gifts at my feet. My mother leaned on the doorway and smiled as she looked at me all excited. Chyna passed me different gifts as I looked at the La Perla lingerie and different things for the house they got me. Benji was about to get the business tonight when we flew to New York.

"Thanks, y'all. I really appreciate y'all for doing this for me."

"You're welcome—now get your makeup and hair done because we're running behind schedule."

There was a knock at the door, and my mother went to answer it. She returned with a gold envelope and handed it to me. I looked at her strangely but took the envelope. Sliding my finger to break the seal, I pulled the paper out of the envelope and started to read it.

WIZ,

Today is the start of forever, and I can't wait to call you my wife. All that we've been going through in life has prepared us for this moment. All the failed relationships, heartbreaks, and nights you've cried yourself to sleep was in preparation for me. Allah knew what he was doing, and when you least expected it, I shot into your life (No pun intended) Today, you're becoming my wife, and I promise to love you with all of me. I'm not gonna get too deep because I still have my vows. Just know you're my queen, and I'm gonna die trying to give you the world.

Your husband,

Benji Johnson

The makeup artist had to keep dabbing my face with a tissue because I was crying like a fool. Benji knew exactly how to make me cry and be an emotional fool over him. I thought I was doing pretty good at keeping my emotions in check, and here he goes and drops a letter off that makes me bawl like a baby.

"What happened?" Chyna asked as she got her makeup done.

I sniffled and put the letter back in the envelope. "Your brother just knows how to make me turn the waterworks on."

Me and Benji, or should I say Benji, decided that we shouldn't have bridesmaids and groomsmen. Besides Chyna, I didn't have friends, and Benji just had JoJo, so Chyna was the maid of honor, and JoJo was his best man. I didn't know if JoJo was going to show because he had a lot going on. If he didn't come, I wasn't going to get on his case about it. I understood that he was going through a lot right now.

"Aww, your hubby." She laughed.

"When is your wedding?" Aaliyah questioned as she got her makeup done. She wasn't in the wedding, but I guess she wanted to look good to sit in the crowd. It wasn't really a crowd either. It was my parents, brother, Kash, Benji's aunt, and Aaliyah.

Chyna messed with her nails and shrugged. "We haven't set a date, and I'm not rushing to. Ohh, what's with you and your new man?" Chyna asked her.

She sighed. "He's been acting weird, and I hadn't seen him in a few days. I've called him, and all I get is his voicemail." She sighed.

"That's a nigga that you don't need," I spoke up. "Get you someone who will call your phone until they get the voicemail."

"Preach, bride to be," the makeup artist said, and we laughed.

Two hours away, and my hair and makeup were done. My dress was this beautiful slick mermaid-style dress. It was sleeveless, but I added some lace sleeves to it. My heels were red, but you couldn't see them because my dress was so long. Chyna and my mother laced the back up as I looked into the mirror and wanted to cry. I was really about to be someone's wife. My hair was styled in finger waves to give me a classic look. Along with my red lipstick, I looked like I was out of an old Hollywood movie.

"You look gorgeous, baby girl." My father walked into the room and hugged me. "Just like a princess."

"Thank you, Daddy! Is Benji out there?"

"I'm out here, Ley," Benji called from the other side of the door. Chyna came through with the tissue to catch the tears that were threatening to fall on my freshly beat face.

"He followed me over here, but I convinced him to wait until you walk down the aisle." My father chuckled, and I smiled.

"Love you, baby!" I called out to him.

"Love you too, Wiz."

My father hugged me again, and poor Chyna was on tissue duty with the way she kept catching those tears. My father had raised me all my life, and now he was handing me over to be a man's wife, his everything for the rest of our lives.

"We're coming out, Benji, so you need to go wait at the altar," Chyna scolded. "Oh bro, you killing it," she said when she peeked her head out the door.

"Thanks. I'll be waiting," he said, and she waited until she saw him walk out the door.

We walked to the door, and I looked out at the beach. The sun was setting in this beautiful orange hue. They had put down a hard floor as the aisle so I could wear heels and wouldn't fall due to the sand. Benji was standing there in a cream suit with a pair of Balmain loafers on. His dreads were styled in a nice up-do, and he looked so handsome. He kept messing with his one signature dread that he always messed with. My mother and Aaliyah kissed me as they went to sit in the few seats that were out there.

"Congratulations, Leyanna; you look gorgeous." I heard a voice behind me and turned. It was JoJo in a similar suit as Benji's.

I wrapped my arms around him and hugged him tightly. "JoJo, you made it!"

"I wouldn't miss this shit for the world."

"Congrats, Leyanna," Renee said as she held a sleeping Jolie. I kissed Jolie on the cheek and rubbed her hair. Poor baby had been through so much, and yet they managed to come and celebrate my day with me.

"I'm happy you came," Chyna said and hugged her brother for a few seconds. "I love you, JoJo."

"I love you too, Mookie," he said and kissed her on the forehead.

The event coordinator put a few more seats out there for them, and Renee and Jolie went to take their seats while JoJo stood next to Benji. Benji's face was so shocked as they shared a hug together.

"You ready for this?" my father squeezed my hand, and I looked into his eyes.

"I'm ready, Daddy!"

Chyna went out first with her bouquet and stood on my side. As soon as me my father stepped out, "I Wanna Be Close" by Avant started to play as I walked down the aisle.

I'll let you know my love is just that strong. And for you. never just ain't that long.

Tears started to come down my eyes as I listened to the song while I looked at Benji. He wiped tears that came down his face. He had to look away a few times because he was tearing up. Chyna was using tissue to wipe her own eyes as she watched me walk to her brother. I held on tightly to my father's arm because as soon as we got to the bottom, he would be giving me away to Benji, who I would confide in and look to when I had problems, and who would be my everything.

"Who gives this woman away?"

My father helped me up the step and backed up.

"I do. Her father," he said and took a seat next to my mother. They both held hands as they watched Benji take my hand and help me the rest of the way. I reached up and wiped the tear that slid down his cheek. The officiant continued with the wedding, and then when he got to the vows, I knew I wasn't going to finish without crying like a fool.

"Benji, I vow to protect, love, and care for you, 'til death do us part is what I believe, baby. There's a lot of things that are uncertain with our future, but knowing that you'll be beside me as my husband makes me feel so much more certain that the future will be a great one. I love you so much that sometimes it hurts me, and I wonder if it's healthy. Then, I see you return the same love I feel for you, and I know that the love I have for you is healthy. You came into my life when everything in my life was crazy. You didn't judge me, although you did act stank." Everyone started laughing as I used this as my chance to sniffle. "I promise to respect your values, even if we don't share the same ones. I want to be your wife forever, and I wouldn't want to take this journey with anyone else."

Benji held my hand and slipped on a diamond wedding band that matched my engagement ring; it was so beautiful that I wanted a minute to fawn over it, yet we were in the middle of a wedding.

"Leyanna, since my mother passed, there hasn't been anyone who could fill that void. I didn't think anyone could fill that void. The only woman I admired and worshipped and vowed to protect was killed, and I thought I had lost a piece of me. Then you came around and filled that void, and I didn't want you to. You never stopped showing that you were down for me and cared about me. Baby, I love the shit out of you, so much that it pains me sometimes. When I sit and think about us, I think of all the kids you gonna give me, the holidays—and I don't even celebrate holidays. For you, I would do all of that and more. I love you, Leyanna Johnson," he said, and I was sobbing like a fool.

I slipped the rose gold wedding band onto his huge finger. This ring was the least I could do for him, especially after all he had done for me. Anytime I needed something for the boutique, he went into his pocket and handled it for me. Financial aid was a thing of the past because Benji took on paying for my tuition along with Chyna's. I had a nice jeep and clothes that I couldn't even afford to buy. I also had a peace of mind knowing that my man wanted me and only me.

"I present to you, Mr. and Mrs. Benji Johnson," the officiant announced, and we jumped over the broom.

We stopped, as Benji reached down and cupped my face while we engaged in a knee-buckling kiss. I was Mrs. Benji Johnson!

26

SOLACE

I WALKED out of the police station and laughed because I had acted like a fool in there. They wanted to speak to me for questioning since Lilly died in her sleep a few weeks ago. At first, I was going to duck and dodge them, then I thought it may make me look guilty as hell. I went in there and cried like a baby when they told me. They should have handed me an Oscar or something because my performance was just that good. They let me leave, and now I was on my way to Aaliyah's place. She had been calling me, and I'd been ignoring her ass. I didn't need her getting on my nerves right now. She kept begging for this car, and I barely had enough to swing her rent this month. BMS had fully kicked GB in the mud.

No connect wanted to even fuck with us because they were afraid their product would be stolen. You know what that did to me? Screwed me over because I had to pay niggas their money back out of mine to avoid being murked when I stepped out the door. I didn't even have enough to get me a damn hotel room. Thankfully, I had bought my car in full when I was making that bread. I needed to move into getting this nigga Kash back quickly.

He thought he was going to come into my life and live good? Nah, he had something coming for him.

Pulling into Aaliyah's driveway, I walked into the house, and she was sitting on the couch with her phone to her ear.

"Girl, let me call you back." She sucked her teeth and put all her attention to me. "You finally decide to come home," she snapped and went into the kitchen.

What the fuck just happened? Aaliyah never threw attitudes with me or questioned where I'd been. She was giving me a different Aaliyah, and I wasn't feeling the shit one bit. She returned with a glass of wine and returned to sitting on the couch with the TV on.

"I had business to handle," I told her, not wanting to give away too much.

"Solace, I deserve way more than what we have going on. You come and go as you please and then try to distract me with clothes and small shit. Where's the car I asked for? Exactly."

Nah, this bitch was in here channeling another chick I was fucking with. Those were the ones who pissed me off with their attitudes and the rolling of the neck. Not Aaliyah; she was a good girl.

"I'm working on getting the shit for you. Why the fuck you rushing me?" I barked, upset that she was even doing this shit right now.

"Broken promises, humph." She rolled her eyes and sipped her drink.

I plopped down beside her and tried to touch her, but she moved away. "My friend hooked me up with a job, so I won't be living here too much longer," she decided she wanted to spring on me.

"I got you this place. Why you leaving?"

"Because the landlord stopped by and told me how you haven't paid him in two months. I'm not paying for this hell hole.

You can have it, and don't think I didn't see you with another chick last week, because I did."

"What the fuck are you talking about?"

This was going left because I needed her to unknowingly lure Chyna back to this crib. Kash didn't think he was getting off easy, did he? I had been gone two weeks and came back to a bitch that thought she was in charge. If I didn't need her, she would have gotten the same treatment that Lilly did.

"I'm just sick of this and I deserve better."

"Aaliyah, I love you, baby, and I don't want nobody else. Let's go pick out a car tomorrow."

She turned and looked at me skeptical. "I'm still getting my own place."

"That's fine. We need something better. Staying here ain't the move," I tried to convince her. "I found this high rise, and I want us to live in it together."

"Together?" She gasped.

"Yeah, that's why I haven't paid the rent on this place," I lied, and she looked at me with wide eyes. Bitches were so easily manipulated. Just like that, I had her right where I needed her.

"Babe, you know how excited I am? Can we get my car now?" She jumped up and down.

"Tomorrow morning... You cooked?"

She nodded her head and went to go get me a plate. I had her exactly where I wanted. I had to implement my plan before she thought she was moving into my new crib.

27

CHYNA

BENJI AND LEYANNA were in New York on their honeymoon. It sucked that they couldn't go too far because Benji had a job to fulfill. I had been opening the shop and closing it for her. Lord knows I didn't need her to come back screaming on me. The wedding was so beautiful, and I still had to slap myself because I couldn't believe my brother now had a wife, and his wife was Leyanna. If there was any marriage that I thought would survive, it was theirs. They both didn't give up easily, and neither of them were willing to throw in the towel when they argued. They must have thought I was a wedding planner and now personal damn assistant.

Benji gave me a budget for a beach house for them. He didn't want nothing big, just two or three bedrooms for them. He wanted to be able to step on the beach from their house, so I was working with his realtor in finding that for him. Since I wasn't working at the store, I figured I could do this much for them. I was sitting in the office going over the few houses that the realtor had sent me. The first one was the house, and I needed to call and put an offer on it before it got snatched up. I sent her an email instead.

Baby Kash was with his grandparents, and Kash was upstairs. He had been acting weird since the wedding, and I didn't know why. Since I finished working in the office, I figured we could have a date night. Our son was away, and it was just us. I walked upstairs and stopped when I heard him on the phone.

"I feel like I need to tell her, Tike," I heard him say. Now, this nigga better not had another bitch because I was gonna bust up in this room and fuck him up. I couldn't hear what Tike was saying, so I was listening to a one-sided conversation.

"She gonna hate me for this shit. At the wedding, I felt guilty as fuck for this shit."

What was he so nervous about? I couldn't understand why he was so upset. I prayed he didn't cheat on me. My heart couldn't take him doing me wrong right now. We had a son and were engaged.

"Bruh, how the fuck I'm gonna sit and talk about how I killed her mother at dinner? The shit is fucked up because when we first met, I put two and two together and held it from her all this time."

My heart stopped when he said that. I felt like all the air was knocked out of my chest, and I couldn't breathe. I gripped the staircase railing as I tried to gather all my strength. Did he just say that he killed my mother? Did I lay down with the man who was responsible for killing my mother?

"Whhhyyyyyyyy?" I screeched because I couldn't move. My legs wouldn't allow me to move and walk into our bedroom—the room we shared many secrets in, yet he seemed to keep one secret away from me.

Kash burst out the door with the phone in his hand and looked at me. I didn't have to explain because he already knew. The pain that was etched on his face was evident from that.

"Why would you take her away from us?" I screamed as I bent down while holding the railing. The room was spinning, and I felt like breathing was getting harder to do.

"Princess, I wan—"

"Don't you dare call me princess!" I screamed and lunged myself at him. Punches, kicks, and slaps were being thrown everywhere, and he just accepted it. It was like he had been holding this for a while and now felt relieved that the secret was out. "I trusted you, and you kept this secret from me!"

My arms, legs, and chest were aching as I backed up from him. I looked at him with so much pain on my face. Turning around, I jogged down the stairs and grabbed my car keys. He chased behind me pleading.

"Chyna, I wanted to tell you. I didn't kill her on purpose, she was just... there," he stopped and pleaded when he got to the bottom of the stairs.

"You took her away from us! Do you know how hard it was growing up without her? Going through life without her here to guide me. Do you? You don't, because both of your parents are living!" I continued to yell as I grabbed my purse and darted out the door.

"We gotta talk about it! Come back!" he pleaded, and I jumped in my car and pulled out the gates.

As soon as I got out the gates, more tears streamed down my face as I wailed in my car. It was so bad that I had to pull over and let it all out. With trembling hands, I grabbed my cell phone and dialed Benji's number.

"What's good, Mookie?" he answered, laughing. I could hear Leyanna in the background laughing too.

"H..." I couldn't even get the words out.

"Mookie, what the fuck happened?" He grew more concerned. It didn't take Benji much to go from laughing to be serious, especially when it came to me and now his wife.

"He killed Mama," I cried into the phone.

The line grew silent, and I had to look at the phone to see if he was still there. "How'd you find out?"

His question threw me off. Did he know this entire time? Had he known the entire time and didn't feel the need to tell me? "Y... you knew?"

"I found out a few months ago."

"Why didn't you tell me! He killed our mother, and you didn't do anything like a pussy!" I screamed.

When it came to Benji, I had the utmost respect for him and would never disrespect him. However, right now I didn't care who he was.

"Because you loved the nigga and got knocked up by him. If you kept your legs closed and didn't get knocked up, I could have murked him without all this other shit. He's your child's father!" he barked, and I jumped. He wasn't even in my face, and I could still feel his presence.

I ended the call and did eighty on the highway back home. There was nothing I could say or do to try and find the light in this situation. Not even my son could make me feel better at this time. I killed the engine and walked into the house. My aunt was sleeping, and I ran up to my room and slammed the door. Throwing myself across my bed, I just cried. I cried because I had a baby with the man who killed his son's grandmother. My entire heart felt like it was broken in a million pieces right now, and nothing could change it.

$$\$\$\$$$

It had been a few weeks since I found out about Kash killing my mother. I hadn't reached out or spoke to him. His mother dropped our son off and questioned what was going on. All I could do was tell her to ask her son and close the door in her face.

It pained me to do that to her, yet seeing her face made me think of the relationship I was denied with my mother because of her son. The holidays were coming, and I wasn't in the mood to be happy and celebrate. My aunt ended up going home because she claimed that I was keeping secrets from her, and she didn't need the stress during her pregnancy.

I was trying to protect her and the baby by not telling her what I knew. If I told her what I knew, she would for sure put stress on her baby. It was just me and Baby Kash in the house, and this was what I needed. The curtains were drawn, and my car was pulled into the driveway to look as if no one was home. Kash called my phone day in and day out from different numbers that I kept blocking. There was nothing he could say, do, or show me that would make this situation alright with me. He was dead to me, and we couldn't be in a relationship. How could we get married and raise our child when I knew what he did? There was no way I could act like this didn't exist and try to rebuild our relationship.

Leyanna had come back and was consumed with finding their dream home, the boutique, and school. She came over and held me as I cried, but I told her she needed to handle her things first. Benji wanted a home to come to when he finished up in New York. She needed to worry about her husband's needs and just allow me to sulk in my house. My son's whining deterred me from my thoughts as I looked at him sitting up. Baby Kash was six months old. He was sitting up, teething, and fussing all the time, yet he was the only thing that caused me to smile these days. College was the least of my problems, so I decided to take a year off and see if I wanted to return after the year was up.

When Benji got the call, he barked on me and made threats that he couldn't keep. I knew he felt guilty for keeping this secret away from me. How could I focus on school right now? Every day when my feet touched the floor, I felt a pain in my chest. That pain was there because of my son's father.

"Chy, where are you?" I heard Leyanna call and wiped the tear that slid down my cheek.

"In my room."

I heard her heels, and she walked into the room a few seconds later. She went straight for the baby and kissed him.

"How you feeling?" She kicked her heels off and climbed into bed with me.

"Trying to move forward... but how?"

"Put one foot in front of the other. You have to think of this little chunker right now." She kissed him on his chubby cheeks. "What are you guys going to do as far as co-parenting?"

"I can't do this right now, Ley," I mumbled.

I couldn't sit here and think of co-parenting, like the situation I was in was normal. It wasn't like he cheated on me and we decided to split and just co-parent our son. He killed my mother and altered my entire life. Benji was a hitman and could be killed or jailed anytime he was on a job. Our lives could have been different if my mother was alive. What if Benji went to college and got an education? When my mother was killed, it forced him to grow up too fast and put his life on the back burner for me.

"Whenever you feel like you are ready, I'll be here."

I nodded my head and turned to look at her. "What's going on with you, Mrs. Johnson?" I laughed.

"The buyers accepted our offer, so now we need to focus on moving and selling his old place."

"I don't know why y'all didn't just live in that house."

"We want it to be both of ours, and it's a new beginning in our new place. Benji hasn't answered his phone yet, so I'm waiting to tell him the news."

"How many bedrooms is it?"

"Three bedrooms. There's an office space downstairs, so I'm glad because it doesn't take up a bedroom."

"Do you think... never mind," I said.

"Tell me, Chy," she pushed.

"Nothing, Ley."

She nudged me to tell her. "Come on, tell me. I had to find out from Benji that you took the year off for school. I don't want to find out from him about this."

"I just was going to ask if maybe I could stay with y'all once y'all are in the new house."

"Is that even a question? You're family, and you and this cutie are always welcome. What you gonna do with this place?"

"Honestly... I don't care."

"You're just over it, huh?" Leyanna laughed, and I had to stifle one too. She was saying anything but the truth right now.

"Yes. I just don't want to be in this house alone. Even if Benji isn't here right now, being under his roof will make me feel close to him."

"I understand, boo." She reached out and hugged me. We sat and watched Netflix for the rest of the day. Leyanna even changed into some pajamas and returned to the bed with me and Baby Kash. It felt good knowing I had her in my corner. Aaliyah had been wanting to hang out, but I just needed time to deal with all of this right now.

28

BENJI

"YEAH, I MISS YOU TOO, BABE," I told Leyanna as she whined about how much she missed me. I missed her like shit and wanted to be with her right now.

The more I was out here, the more I realized that I couldn't do this shit no more. I had a wife, sister, and nephew that depended on me now. Chyna was hurt over finding out about our mother. That shit broke me up to hear her calling me and crying about it. It broke my heart to keep that secret from her. Kash had hit me and asked me to speak to Chyna because he really loved her and wanted to marry her. The nigga had a few screws loose if he thought he and Chyna were going to be able to play happy family.

"Babe?" Leyanna broke me from my thoughts.

"Yeah, what's up?"

"When is this going to be over?" she questioned.

I sighed because I thought this would be easy, and it wasn't. I was paid ten million to take this nigga down, and I couldn't back out now. In the future, I wanted to have kids with my wife and live happily. Doing this shit wasn't going to assure that, so I had to step away from this.

"Baby, I wish it was sooner than later. But this is the last one, I promise."

"For how long?" she shot back, skeptical.

"For the rest of our lives. I'm gonna do another sneaker store when I get home."

It was crazy how I could hear the smile in her voice. "I don't want you to th—"

"This is my choice. I wanna sleep beside my wife every night, no more trips," I promised her.

"I'm so happy, baby!" She squealed. "Chy wants to move into the new place," she also informed me.

"She know her and Baby Kash are welcome. Not an issue."

"I told her that," she replied.

I saw the nigga walking down the block alone. This was the first time he had been alone the entire time I'd been here. The person who hired me told me that it would take me a few months to complete this job. I was getting excited thinking that I could be on my way back to Miami sooner than later.

"Wiz, I'll hit you up later... love you."

I didn't wait for her to say it back because I ended the call and emerged from my car. I acted like I was getting a coffee from the newsstand when he passed. This nigga was always with an entourage, and now he was by himself. Trying not to look obvious, I walked down the block and drank this nasty ass coffee. When he turned the corner, he got into a Lincoln Town Car. Acting like I was heading into the bank, I realized that he was meeting with a cop. I could spot a cop from anywhere, and this nigga was definitely snitching. If this nigga was snitching, then that meant they were watching his moves. Quickly, I called my accountant and then dipped out the bank.

As I was driving back to my condo, I got a phone call.

"Yo."

"I just a transfer confirmation on the money I sent. What happened?"

I ended the call and tossed the phone out the window. These niggas were on some next shit. I never spoke business over the phone. He knew that, so I didn't know why he would even try to attempt to have this conversation via phone call. Sending my accountant a message to pass along, I went and grabbed my shit to get to the airport. If I wasn't smart and didn't calculate my moves before I made them, I could have been caught up in these niggas' mess. Money meant shit to me, but it didn't mean more than my freedom, and I wasn't about to get caught up with this shit.

"What's good, nigga?" JoJo answered the phone. He sounded much better than the last time we spoke.

"We out. We done."

"You sure about this?" he asked.

"Very sure."

"Then we done," he said and ended the call.

That's all I needed to head to the airport and get home to my wife. It was crazy how life worked and how I was anticipating staying for a little while longer to get the job done. I think Allah was part of the reason why all of this fell into place for me at this moment. I turned the lights off in the condo and went to head to the airport.

Hailing a cab, I bought a ticket for the first flight that was heading out. It was departing in an hour, so I had enough time to get through security and board the plane. In my head, all I thought about was Leyanna and being next to my wife. Then, I couldn't wait to hold Mookie and let her get the hurt she was feeling out. We made it through the worst shit, so this too would pass.

$$$

By the time the flight landed, it was late and dark. Leyanna had probably tried to call me, and I couldn't answer because my phone was on airplane mode. I was excited to get home and see my wife. Knowing her, she would probably be sitting at the kitchen table with that damn laptop. I sat in the back of the cab and thought about what I was going to say when I saw Mookie. Since she called me crying, I hadn't seen her face to face. This was the exact opposite of what I wanted for my sister when I moved her down here. The reason I got her away from New York was because of the ratchet chicks she hung out with. I was certain she wouldn't be pregnant and dropping out of school for some nigga.

Never did I think she would move down here, find our mother's murderer, and get knocked up by the nigga. Shit like this just didn't happen in life, and here we were living the shit. Mookie took the year off, and I knew she wouldn't be returning back. College wasn't her thing, and she told me that, yet I forced her into applying for college and taking those SAT exams. I thought her dreams were owning a clothing store, so I made that happen, and she ended up letting Leyanna take over it. What the fuck was up with her?

The cab pulled in front of the crib, and I reached in my pocket to pay him before I got out and slammed the door behind me. The light in the living room was on, so I used my key and opened the door. Mookie was in the kitchen with Baby Kash sitting on the counter in some baby seat. Leyanna was sitting at the kitchen table while Mookie was quizzing her for a test.

Leyanna looked up, and her face dropped when she saw it was me.

"Babbbbyyyyy!" she screamed and jumped into my arms while showering me with a bunch of kisses everywhere. "What are you doing here?" she asked in a high-pitched voice.

Mookie stood there with her arms folded and a smile on her

face. Seeing how hype Leyanna was to see me would make anybody laugh, smirk, or smile.

"I'm out," was all I said, and she hugged me tightly around the neck.

"And I'm pregnant," she whispered in my ear. When she said that, I damn near dropped her, and my knees were buckling. She didn't just tell me that she was carrying my seed, did she?

"Ley, don't play me."

"She's not lying. We came from the doctor's this afternoon." Mookie came from behind the kitchen counter with the baby in her hands.

He was fighting her, and she was trying to control him. "I still didn't get my period, and I went to speak to my doctor. He did a blood test, and it came back that I'm pregnant."

"Nahhh," was all that left my mouth as Leyanna got down and led me to the couch. I plopped down and looked at my wife. "You really carrying my seed?"

"Yep. Two months pregnant and didn't even know it." She giggled.

In her face, I could tell she was nervous and excited at the same time. "Wiz, you gonna finish school and continue to run your business and shit. I'm not gonna make you barefoot and pregnant, you heard?"

She climbed into my lap and laid her head on me. "Baby, we'll deal with all of this. But I want to tell you something."

"What's that?"

"You did something for me... for us." She placed her hand on her flat stomach. "I want to convert to Islam," she revealed.

When she said that shit, I damn near fell out. What the fuck were they trying to do? Kill a nigga with surprises?

"Ma, as much as I want you to do that, I know you're doing it for me. When you truly want to do it, then we'll do it." I kissed her on the lips.

She nodded her head and crawled up further on me. It was as if she didn't want to let me out of her sight, and I was cool with that. My wife was my world, and being here with her meant a lot to me.

"I'm going home. He needs a bath and is tried." Mookie broke up our cuddle session when she walked by.

"We need to talk tomorrow," I warned her, and she waved me off.

I guess she was still in her feelings, but I was going to have a talk with her ass tomorrow about what she was doing with herself. Baby Kash deserved the world from her, and she needed to give it to him. Tough shit happened to tough people, so she needed to toughen up and deal with this shit.

29

KASH

CHYNA HADN'T SPOKE to me since she found out about me killing her mother. I couldn't eat, sleep, or move without her being here with me. I couldn't see my son, and I missed the shit out of him. Chyna warned my mother about bringing my son around me when she had him. Imagine knowing you could go hop in a car and head to your parents' house to see your son, but you couldn't because they wanted to respect Chyna's wishes. My mother continued to probe about why we were in this fucked up space. How was I supposed to tell her that I killed my fiancée's mother, yet I didn't know Chyna or her mother when I did it? I had to explain how I continued to get my feelings involved even after discovering that I had killed her moms.

After Benji's wedding, I had been thinking about it more and more. I could tell she sensed something was wrong with me and couldn't place her finger on it. Tike had proved to be a thorough-bred on my team. I had opened up to him because I felt like he could keep shit on the low. When I was in the room, I was pacing the floor and venting. I didn't think she would be coming upstairs because she had been in the office all day. The look of pain that was on her face hit me like a bunch of bullets. Knowing that I was the reason my princess was in pain tore me up. How could we move past this? If I had to take a guess, we couldn't move on from this. Chyna would never be able to trust me, and without trust, there was no relationship.

Today was Flex's birthday, and his death was never easy on me, especially sitting in my crib all alone. My mother had been calling me all day to see if I was straight, and I hadn't answered. It had been me and this bottle of Henny since last night. The only time I got up was to piss in the plants that sat near the living room and grab another bottle from the bar to sip on while looking at SportsCenter. Tike knew I needed a minute because he refrained from hitting my line about work. He knew I had trust that he would handle shit in my absence.

My son and Chyna meant the world to me, and if I couldn't have them, then I didn't want shit. I built BMS from the ground up, and I would hand this entire shit over if Chyna wanted me to. If that's what it took to get her and my son back in my life, then that's what I would do for her. I missed hearing my son screaming at the top of his lungs because he thought it was funny to scare his mother. Shit had me with tears coming down my cheek as I thought about him. I missed hearing Chyna complaining about me leaving my laundry on the bathroom floor. She had to know my feelings were true for her. What other woman did I put a whole salon in my basement for?

I sniffled and gripped the bottle when I heard the doorbell ring. It must have been someone who security approved because they wouldn't have made it through my gates. Staggering over to the door, I swung it open, and I thought my eyes were playing tricks on me. Chyna was standing there in the flesh.

She pushed me aside and walked into the house. "It smells like piss in here. What the hell?" She looked around like she was trying to find out where it was coming from.

"I pissed in the bushes," I slurred.

"And he has the nerve to be drunk," she mumbled as she stood there with her hand on her hips. "Where's your cell phone?"

I pointed to the living room, and she went to grab the phone. "Why you need my jack?"

"Your mother has called you more than a dozen times, Kairo. Your father was in an accident, and she's been calling to tell you."

I couldn't formulate words because I was grabbing the keys off the foyer table. Chyna quickly grabbed the keys from me and shook her head. "There's already been one accident, and we don't need another one. I'll drive you," she suggested.

"How?"

"Some man was driving on the wrong side of the street and they collided. Your father wasn't responsive when they took him to the hospital. Your mother said he's awake now and just wants you there."

This shit was crazy, and my chest was pounding a million miles an hour. "H... he gonna be good?" was all I could mumble.

"We'll see when we get to the hospital. Can't say the same thing about my mother," she added as we walked out the house.

"I'm sorry," I told her, and she ignored me.

"You're sorry." She scoffed and started the car. "Let me go take your sorry and pour it on my mother's grave to revive her," she sarcastically stated. "I'd rather you not talk to me the entire ride."

I was so fucked up that I couldn't hold a conversation if I wanted to. The most I could do is say a few words without repeating the same thing over and over again.

"Ch—"

"Wanna ride to your mother in a cab?"

I just sat back and kept quiet while we rode to Key West to see if my father was straight.

$$$

By the time we arrived at the hospital, I had sobered up. Chyna didn't say anything to me the entire ride. It was as if she didn't want to be here with me at this moment. I started to tell her to take a cab back and that she didn't have to drive me home, yet she chirped the alarm and headed into the hospital, so I followed behind her. The nurses told us his room number, and we headed there. When I pushed the door open, my father was laid in the bed and looked to be sleeping. My mother was sitting in the chair shaking her leg, something she did when she was nervous. When she laid eyes on me and Chyna, she ran and hugged us both.

"He's sleeping now, but he has a fractured collarbone. Thank God that's all." She sighed a breath of relief.

I walked over and kissed my father on his forehead, then took a seat next to my mother. Chyna stood up and looked at my father. I could tell there was so much she wanted to say, and it was probably driving her crazy.

"Are you guys back together?" my mother asked us as she looked from Chyna to me to give her the answer.

Chyna shook her head no. "We're not."

That shit hurt a nigga's soul bad. I couldn't say I was surprised because she let me know that she had no interest in being back with me ever in life. My mother nodded her head, and I sighed.

"Y'all need to fix it. Life is too short for the foolishness... What about Peanut?" she said, talking about the baby. She called him her little peanut, and now she and my pops called him that.

"Life is very short, especially when it's taken from you," Chyna said and left out the room.

My mother sat looking puzzled by what Chyna meant by that. I sat back in the chair and allowed her to be alone. It made no sense to add more fuel to the fire by following behind her. My mother held my hand as she said a prayer for all of us. My father's and mother's prayers could move water and shake mountains. When you had parents that constantly prayed for your well-being, you were blessed whether you knew it or not.

We sat in the room for two hours, and Chyna still hadn't come back. I assumed she headed back home in a cab or my whip. I got up to stretch my legs from sitting so much.

"Kairo?" my father called me, and I turned around. His voice was groggy, and his eyes were squinted from the lights. I turned them lower and pulled my chair close to his bed.

"Pops, how you feeling?"

"Like a bus ran me over." He laughed and choked for a bit. "You didn't need to rush down here for me."

"Pops, I'm always going to rush anywhere for you and Mama. You crazy, man," I joked and hit him lightly.

"They keeping me, so take your mama home. She gonna have a crook in her neck," he tried to tell me, but my mother wasn't in a deep enough sleep.

"Myles, I'm not going anywhere tonight. I'll stay right here with my crook and all," her stubborn self said.

"So stubborn." My father shook his head. "Go get her some food and something to drink."

"Now that, I'll take," she added.

"I'll be back," I told them and walked down the hallway. When I passed the guest lounge, Chyna was laying across two chairs and shivering. All this time, I thought she had left and was already home by now.

Taking my shirt off, I placed it over her and walked to the machines with just my wife beater on. "Why?"

I turned around, and she was stirring from her sleep and sitting up. Turning around, I took a seat across from her. Looking in her eyes, I had to tell her the truth. Even if we didn't have a future together, she had to know I didn't do this shit on purpose.

"I was young and needed to get out the city. It wasn't good for me... us," I corrected myself. She crossed her legs and allowed me to tell her everything that went down the day I took her mother's life. When I was finished, she had tears coming down her eyes as she sobbed into her hand.

"She was our world, Kash," she whimpered. I tried to get up to comfort her, and she held her hand up. "Don't touch me!"

"Princess, you think I really wanted to kill your mother? I've lived with that shit every day, and when I found out about you... I wanted to tell you, I really did."

"Why would you make me fall in love with you and have your son? That shit isn't fair to me." She sobbed. "I would have been better off not knowing what you did."

"It wasn't fair to you, I know."

"It wasn't fair to us." She pointed at her stomach.

Did she just tell me that she was pregnant again? Nah, she didn't just tell me this shit because I was about to lose my mind if she did.

"You pregnant?"

"I can't keep this baby, and I won't," she told me. "The baby isn't even a year old, and we're not together."

On one hand, I understood where she was coming from. Then again, if everybody got rid of their kid because they weren't with their nigga, then we would be damn near extinct as a species.

"Chy, please think about this shit... but if you do it, I won't be mad," I told her.

"This is what I have to do. What I look like having two kids at twenty years old, no college, and not with their father? Benji would kill me before anything. It hurts because Leyanna is pregnant and we could be pregnant together, but I know what I have to do."

"If you feel like you have to do this, then you got my support," I said.

She rolled her eyes and wiped the tears out of her eyes. "You'll support anything I do because you feel guilty."

She was right. I wasn't the happiest about the abortion and wished she would reconsider. It would break my parents' hearts to know that they wouldn't be able to meet their second grandchild. I knew I would have to keep this shit from them and let Chyna do what she was gonna do.

"Tell your father I'll be praying for him. I need to get home to the baby."

"Take my whip, and I'll catch a cab back home or drive my mother's whip," I told her, and she walked out of the guest lounge. I put my head in my hands because my past was interfering with my future. Because I did dirt, it was coming back to me ten times worse than before.

30

LEYANNA

I COULDN'T BELIEVE that I was carrying my husband's child. After all the fussing I did about being an independent woman and not being his baby making machine, I was carrying a piece of both of us inside of me. We both were going to be parents, and I was so excited to tell my parents. We were leaving the doctor's office, and Benji had tears in his eyes as he listened to our baby's healthy heartbeat on the machine. We actually created a human being together. There was something about being pregnant; you found everything to be cute. For the most part, I wasn't having those morning sickness symptoms, which was how I ended up to be two months and hadn't even known.

We were on our way to my father's house to tell him and my mother about our new family member that was going to be making an appearance in seven months. When I thought about it, it was crazy that I was carrying our child when we got married. At least I'd be a married woman when I gave birth. I had to chuckle at my own thought. As for the boutique, I was going to continue to run it along with going to school. When I got too far along, I was going to transfer all my classes to online.

Right now, I was taking a few classes online and going to the rest. I made my schedule like that so I could work at the boutique during the morning because Khloe worked a second job in the morning.

"You excited about this, babe?" I asked him.

Since finding out that we were expecting, he was the happiest he'd ever been. Besides the fact that Chyna was hurting over what Kash did, life was good for us. We closed on our house and were moving things to and from the new house.

"Yeah, I can't wait to see that stomach pop out." He laughed.

"I can wait. You gonna tie my shoe for me?"

He laughed and nodded his head as we continued to drive to my father's house. Chyna decided that she didn't want to move in with us. She swindled Benji into renting her a condo right on the beach. I guess it made more sense than having a huge house in this gated community. It was two bedrooms and enough for her and Baby Kash. Benji would do anything she asked because he truly felt guilty for not telling Chyna when he found out. I understood the position he was in and why he did it. He was honestly trying to keep the peace between them.

We pulled up to my father's house and stepped out. My mother was walking out when we pulled out. She stopped and waited until we parked.

"Hey, baby girl; what you doing here?"

I hugged her and stepped back. "I told y'all I was going to come around more."

"You did say that... hey, Benji," she greeted and hugged Benji. "Your father didn't cook anything, so I'm running out to get some pizza. Y'all want something?"

"We're not staying that long. We just have to tell y'all something," I said, and she grew concerned.

"None of y'all dying, right?" She pointed at both me and Benji.

"Nah, nothing like that," Benji told her, and she sighed a breath of relief.

"Okay. I guess I can wait a few minutes. If Zack gets huffy, you better tell him that you're the reason," she joked as we walked back inside.

My father was just coming downstairs when he saw me. "Hey, Ley. Everything good?"

"Dang, y'all really didn't believe me when I said I was going to start popping up more," I said.

"I'm just joking, baby." He hugged me and gave Benji a hand-shake. "Come in the kitchen." We followed behind him while he made himself something to drink.

"Mama and Daddy, I'm pregnant!" I blurted because I couldn't hold it in any longer.

My mother screamed and jumped up and down. "I knew something when we were tying the back of your dress."

"My stomach flat, Mama," I said, offended.

"Girl, that ass and thighs ain't flat." She laughed.

My father hugged me and Benji with a smile on his face. "I'm excited to have a grandchild. What does mean for school?"

"She's still going to finish. When she has the baby, she'll take some time off, but I'm gonna make sure she keeps up with her work."

My father didn't have a comeback because he liked everything that Benji had to say. We already worked out everything when it came to the new baby.

"We also closed on our new house. You guys can come over whenever you want," I informed them.

My mother gasped. "Where?"

"Right on Miami Beach; soon as I walk out the back door, my feet hit the sand," I told her.

Things were happening for us, and I was so excited. I felt like we did this the right way, and that was why I was content with it all. We were a married couple, bought a home, and now we were going to be welcoming our child in the coming months. God was in the business of blessing us, and I couldn't do anything but keep thanking Him.

"I'm excited for both of y'all," my dad said again. "You are really happy with Benji, and that makes me happy."

Getting my father's full blessing meant the world to me. He was a good judge of character and didn't have much to say about Benji. Since we'd met, he has treated me as a queen and always had my best interest at heart. We'd had some bumps along the road, and we managed to make it work for nobody except us.

31

CHYNA

AALIYAH CALLED me and wanted me to get out the house. After my abortion, I felt like shit and didn't want to be around anyone. I was surprised when I found out I was pregnant. When Leyanna asked me to go with her to the doctor, I decided to make an appointment since we went to the same office. Thankfully, Leyanna was sitting in the waiting area with the baby when I was getting the exam. When the doctor came back and told me that I was pregnant, I was shocked as hell. The last thing I thought was that I was pregnant. I just wanted to get checked up and get on some kind of medicine to help with the terrible cramps I was experiencing during my period. The doctor told me it was possible for a woman to get her period during her pregnancy.

"I'm glad that you decided to come out," she said as we drove from the mall. I was in such a bad funk that I didn't even swipe my credit card.

"Yeah, me too. This car is nice," I complimented her on the Honda her man had bought her. I was glad that he was trying to treat her better. Well, those were her words, not mine.

Since I left Kash in the guest lounge in the hospital, I hadn't heard from him. I think he knew I needed my time and to allow me that. All I sent was a text message letting him know that I did it. He didn't bother to respond back, and I didn't care. Another baby would be stupid as hell for me. Not to mention that I'd be trying to raise two babies as a single mother. When I thought about it, that wasn't what my mother wanted for me. Leyanna agreed to watch the baby so I could clear my head. I hadn't told her or Benji about the abortion. Aaliyah had come and picked me up from the clinic. If I would have told her, she would have been on her little positivity trip she had been on since finding out about her baby.

"Thanks, girl." She smiled and answered her phone.

I looked out the window and thought about what I was doing with my life. What did I truly want to do with myself? It seemed like nothing made me happy these days except when I laid eyes on my baby boy. Nothing outside of him moved me. It was probably because I was so depressed over how things went down between me and Kash. How could the nigga I was in love with be responsible for killing my mother? I heard his story, yet it didn't make it any better.

"Girl, I need to go take my boyfriend this money I've been holding for him. You mind?"

"Do you," I told her, and we headed to her house. Damn, I didn't know this heifer lived in the damn hood.

I wasn't picky and had been raised in the hood myself, yet she was bragging on a house her man was renting for her. The shit was in the hood, and there was a corner store with about ten niggas on every corner. We pulled into a driveway with dead grass, and she killed her engine.

"You staying here or coming?"

Looking around, I decided to come inside with her. She unlocked her door, and we stepped inside. The inside was nice, and she looked to have kept up with it. You definitely would have misjudged her house from looking at the outside.

"Babe, where are you?" she called and put her purse down. "I'm gonna get us some water."

"Where's your bathroom?"

"Around that corner, straight to the back," she told me with her head in the fridge.

I placed my purse down and went to use the bathroom. When I got to the little dingy bathroom, I squatted and pissed. After I was finished, I came out the bathroom and ran right into a man.

"Excuse me," I said and tried to walk around him, but he pushed me up to the wall with this demonic expression plastered on his face. "Get the fuck off of me!" I yelled.

Aaliyah must have heard me and came around the corner. "Solace, what the fuck are you doing?" she yelled.

She tried to push him, and he backslapped her, and she fell to the floor. "Bitch, speak when spoken to!" he barked with spit flying from his mouth.

I shoved him hard and tried to run, and he bust me in the back of my head with something. I fell to the floor and still tried to crawl out away from him. If only I could make it to my bag, then I could call Benji, and this nigga would know not to mess with me.

"You still wanna continue to fuck with me... sit still!" he barked and bust me in the back of my head. Everything was spinning, and the room was getting dark. It wasn't long before I was knocked out cold.

32

SOLACE

"SOLACE, WHY ARE YOU DOING THIS?" Aaliyah's annoying ass screamed with tears running down her face. Her nose was all bloodied because I had punched her in that shit a few times.

I continued to fuck the shit out of Chyna, and she was still unconscious. She was stirring and coming to. It was only a matter of time before she was fully awake, and I could call her punk ass baby father so he could hear what the fuck I was doing. Aaliyah was still in the door crying and screaming.

"Get the fuck out and go make me something to eat!" I barked, and she stood there with tears coming down her eyes.

She wasn't stupid, so I wasn't worried about her going and telling anybody. Matter fact, her ass couldn't be trusted either. I jumped off of Chyna with my hard dick swinging and grabbed Aaliyah by the neck. Dragging her screaming ass, I went and tied her ass to the kitchen chair so she could watch me. Her little ass was fighting back, so it let me know my choice to tie her up was the best thing because she couldn't be trusted. All these months I had been taking care of her, and she was just going to turn on me like it was nothing.

When I got her tied up and punched her a few times, she was out cold. Chyna was fully awake and trying to get off the bed. I shoved her back onto the bed and spread her legs open. Shoving myself inside of her, she screamed, kicked, and tried to bite me. Her little weight was nothing compared to me putting my weight on her.

"Oh God, pleaseee, don't rape me," she begged like I hadn't been fucking her moments before.

"See how this dick slide up in here? I've already hit it when you were out cold." I chuckled and started round two. The three mollies I had popped along with the Red Bull had me wired, not to mention the three hits of coke I had taken minutes before they walked into the house.

Aaliyah kept rambling about how she was going shopping with Chyna. I handed her money to hold for me, and that was how I got her to get back to the apartment. If I knew her, she would drop Chyna off before trying to come back to the crib. I made the shit seem like it was an emergency, which was why she flew her ass over here.

With one hand, I grabbed the burner phone off the dresser and dialed the number I had for Kash.

"Yo." He picked up and I placed it on speaker.

"What's good, nigga? You thought you were going to fuck over GB and I wasn't going to fuck your fiancée?" I cackled into the phone.

"What the fuck? Who the fuck is this?"

"Solace, nigga." I laughed.

"Fuck you, nigga. Playing that phone tag shit," he barked.

"Nah, I'm fucking your girl." I put the phone to her mouth, and she was crying and saying inaudible shit. "Speak, gushy pussy!" I yelled.

"K... Kash, pleaseeee, help me." She sobbed as I continued to fuck her. "Kash, please, he's raping me!" she screamed a blood-curdling scream.

I bust her in the head and she was out again. "Oops, she out again." I laughed.

"Nigga, when I find you, I'm going to fucking put a hot one in your head. Your fucking life is over, bitch!" he was screaming through the phone like I gave a damn about what he was chatting about.

"Yeah, the only thing you gonna find is this bitch's throat cut," I told him and ended the call.

These bitches were about to get the Lilly treatment. After I nutted a few times, I put a handcuff on her wrist and the head-board before going to shower and get some grub. As I was about to walk out the room, I had the urge to slap Aaliyah in the face with my dick, so I did. Bitch was still out cold, so I closed the door and went to get something to eat. I was definitely going to come back for some more when I ate and took a nap.

33

BENJI

"WHAT THE FUCK YOU TELLING ME?" I barked as Kash told me what happened. It didn't matter that Leyanna was laying across me asleep. I jumped up and went into the closet to get dressed with the phone still attached to my ear.

"Yo, Benj, I'm fucked up over this shit. I heard him raping her while he was on the line with me."

When those words left his mouth, I went fucking crazy. I ripped the closet door from the wall and slammed it around the room. The phone had dropped, and Leyanna was sitting in the middle of the bed looking scared.

"B... baby," she called out. "Please, stop, Benji, you're scaring me," she continued to plead with me.

When I continued to fuck up the room, she ran out and went downstairs. I didn't mean to make her scared and fuck her head up, but this nigga really took it there. Why the fuck did he have to come and fuck with my sister? Kash was yelling through the phone as I sat on the edge of the bed and tried to get my mental together.

"Babe," Leyanna called from the doorway.

She looked so scared and innocent that I felt bad that I fucked this whole room up. Walking toward me, she handed me the phone that Kash was screaming on.

"Meet me at your crib in ten minutes."

"I'm already here," he said and ended the call.

"JoJo is on his way," Leyanna said and walked out the room. My wife already knew what time it was and called my right-hand.

That nigga was about to find out who the fuck he had kidnapped and raped. My wife, sister, and aunt were the only women that had my heart and who I would protect. He fucked with one of them, and now he was about to be a dead man. Did he seriously not know what I did for a living? It took no time for JoJo to arrive at the house.

"Somebody kidnapped Mookie," was all I said for right now. If I told him what really went down, we would have the same issues I had right now.

"Who the fuck got her?" he barked.

"Ley, go to your father's house, now!" I barked, and she was already walking in the living room with a sweat suit on.

"I'm going," she said and hugged me. "Be careful, y'all." She looked at us.

We headed out, and I followed Leyanna until she was at her father's house. When she entered, she blew a kiss at me and turned to lock the door. I sped through the streets until we pulled up to the gates of Kash's crib. Usually, you had to wait to go through the gates. This nigga was waiting outside the gate. Popping the locks, he got in the back as we drove to Lemon City.

"Where the fuck this nigga be?"

"I heard he goes to this lounge every night. He supposed to have some money invested in the shit. The last of his money since we fucked his shit up."

"Who told you this?" JoJo questioned.

"I heard from this nigga that wanna get down with BMS."

I shook my head. "This nigga down with you?"

"Hell nah. He wanna get down and will tell anything to be a part. We need to find out where the fuck he got her; he'll go back if he leaves her."

We parked a few blocks from the lounge. It was starting to get dark, and there were people hanging out and selling drugs in front. My mind was on Mookie and if she was alright. Kash kept mumbling shit to himself and punching his hand while we were waiting. It was hard sitting here and not doing nothing. We had to know where this nigga was going and where he had my sister.

"I should have had two of them on her," he mumbled.

"What?" I questioned.

"Chyna told her security guard to stop following her when she left my crib. She didn't want me knowing where the fuck she was. I had the nigga on her, and she caught him and told him she would call the cops on him if he continued."

I shook my head because it sounded just like something Mookie would say. We continued to sit and wait until this nigga pulled up. My eyes were peeled for anything that didn't look right to me.

"Look, that's the little nigga that fuck with him," Kash pointed out. "Niggas say that it's his blood son, but he been denying him for years," he continued.

"It's nine now, and this nigga still hasn't showed up." I looked at my watch.

The little nigga walked across the street and got into the back of a cab. He had two bags of food, it looked like. "I'm following this cab."

"Bet."

We followed the cab two cars back as we drove into the hood. It was a street with dilapidated houses and people sitting outside with beers in their hands. I pulled behind a Ford

Explorer and watched the nigga go to the door of the house. JoJo already jumped out and acted as if he was walking down the street. I didn't have to call and worry about what he was going to do. We had been doing this so long that we trusted each other's moves.

Him and the little nigga chalked up a conversation, then they were walking back to the car. JoJo opened the door and shoved the nigga inside, hitting his head on the side of the car. He closed the door with the nigga sitting in his seat. He got into the back with Kash.

"Man, what the fuck? You said you got cheap good weed." The young stoner was more concerned with getting high.

"Who the fuck in that house?"

"I don't know. He told me he had two bad bitches and couldn't leave, and that they were hungry. I was playing 2K16 with my friends when he said he would pay me a hundred dollars to go get the food and bring it to him."

"Who told you? Who?" Kash slapped him in the back of his head with his gun.

"Chill, chill." He held the back of his head. "Solace."

"Who he in there with?"

"Nobody; he called me because nobody fucking with him because of how he handled GB. I need the money for school, so I do little stuff for him."

I was conflicted on if I wanted to pop this little nigga. Digging in my pocket, I peeled off money and grabbed him by the side of his neck. "You didn't talk to us, you hear. You got a moms?"

"Yeah, and two brothers."

"You wanna come home and find them dead?" I wouldn't do no shit like that, but I wanted to put the fear of Allah into this nigga. "Take this money and leave this street shit alone, you hear me?"

"Y... yeah, I got you." He scrambled out the car.

"Damn, that's cold. His moms and brothers," Kash commented.

Me and JoJo looked at him before JoJo spoke. "Says the nigga that killed his moms."

The houses had back doors, so we agreed we would break up. I was coming through the front, and both Kash and JoJo were covering the back. We got out the car and went to get Mookie. JoJo and Kash went to the back, and as I stood at the front door, I heard them in there, tearing shit up. The front door flew open, and this nigga ran right into me.

"Where the fuck you going?" I asked as I gripped his neck and pushed him back inside the crib. This nigga had white shit all around his nose and shit.

When I walked into the crib, I kicked this nigga in the stomach, and he fell onto the floor. Kash came out the back with Mookie, and she was bruised and bloodied. I took this nigga and looked him in his eyes.

"You fucked with the wrong chick, you hear me?" He didn't say anything because he was trying to fight to get away.

JoJo brought another chick out and laid her on the couch. Mookie was out of it like he had knocked her out or something. Looking at my sister and how she was covered in a blanket with blood on it, I put my hands around his neck and squeezed until I heard something pop. Even then, I couldn't stop choking this nigga. I was squeezing so hard my hand was turning red.

"He gone, Benji," JoJo said and tapped my hand.

I dropped his lifeless body and looked at Mookie in Kash's arms. "I called this doctor I know. He's gonna take care of them at my crib," Kash informed me.

We left out the back door with Mookie and the other chick. Kash sat with Mookie's body on his when we got in the car. The other chick was up and too scared to talk.

"I... I swear I didn't know he was going to do this," she sobbed. "I'm so sorry, Chyna," she wept.

"Didn't know he would do what?" I asked as I watched JoJo jog back to the car. He set that entire crib on fire.

"He... he told me to come home to drop money off, and I did. That's when he took Chyna and beat me and tied me to the chair. I swear I didn't know," she said as her body shook.

I believed she really didn't know what the fuck was going on. She got involved with the wrong nigga, and this is how it ended up here. "We going to his house where the doctor is going to check on you."

"P... please don't kill me, please... I'll leave the city," she continued to beg.

Kash grabbed her face and looked her in the eyes. "If we were going to kill you, then we would have in the crib. Calm down. You're safe."

Taking them to the doctor would be like asking the police to come into our business. I felt that nigga took the easy way out, but my anger wouldn't allow me to stop squeezing his neck. He crossed the line when he fucked with my sister. Whatever beef he had didn't have shit to do with Mookie, and he crossed that line when he called himself bragging about raping her.

34

CHYNA

I OPENED my eyes and looked out the window that had the sun shining through. There was an IV attached to my arm, and my mouth felt like I had cotton in it. My body was so sore that when I tried to sit up, it was painful. Tears slid down my face when I thought about what that sick fuck did to us. He made both of us watch each other have sex with him. For hours, he raped and tortured me. Certain times, I had to black out because the pain was unbearable. Whenever he didn't like what I would say, he would knock me over the head with something. I opened my eyes again and looked around the room. It looked familiar to me from what I could see when I kept opening my eyes.

I tried to move my lips and they hurt. It felt like someone sat and picked the skin off of them. Turning my head away from the window, I winced in pain. Once my head was away from the bright window, I opened my eyes again and tried to look at the other half of the room. The golden accent chair was familiar along with the chaise in the corner. I was in Kash's bed. Trying to get up, I stopped once I felt like someone had just poked me with a knife all over my body.

"Mookie, don't move," Benji said as he walked into the room. I was so groggy that I couldn't make out what happened to me.

"W... water," I managed to mumble to him.

He walked closer and picked up the glass with ice in it. Bending the straw, he inserted it between my lips. I tried to finish the whole glass because I was so thirsty. When the glass was finished, I started to move my lips, and that was when I felt the stitches that were on my lips.

"You have a concussion and have been out for two days... We didn't think you were going to make it," he finally spoke again.

That was when I realized that they had a whole setup of hospital equipment in the room. I didn't need to ask how they got these things because between Benji and Kash, they knew a lot of people.

I wiped the tears from my eyes and continued to cry. It was like it was so vivid in my head that I felt like I was reliving it all over again.

"H... he raped me." I sobbed, and Benji bent over and hugged me while I cried. "That sick fuck raped me!" I continued to scream.

"Mookie, you don't have to worry about him anymore, you hear me? He's in the past and ain't gonna come after you anymore."

Benji wiped my tears, and then another thing came back to me. "Where's Aaliyah?" I panicked.

"She's in the next room. Want me to get her?"

I nodded my head up and down, and he left the room. At first, I thought Aaliyah was a part of this, then when he did the same things to her that he was doing to me, I realized that she wasn't. I had to watch as he punched her in the face a few times.

"Hey, Chyna." Aaliyah walked into the room. Her nose was bandaged up, and she had a cast on her arm.

"We're fucked up, huh?" I chuckled, and she laughed while pulling a chair up to the bed.

"Pretty much. I just want you to know that I'm sorry for putting you through this. If I would have known he was going to do this, I wouldn't have come back to my house. JoJo explained what Solace was capable of, and I just feel so lucky that they came and got us out of the house."

Tears slid down my cheek as they did hers. "I just wish we could turn back the hands of time. Why did he have to do that shit? I feel sick every time I think about it. We'll heal and get through this together." She grabbed my hand.

Aaliyah was shady as shit when I first met her through Leyanna, yet now that I was hanging out with her, I saw that she had changed. She wasn't trying to be my friend under false pretenses; she genuinely wanted a friend. I could tell in her face that she had no clue about Solace's plan that he had concocted.

"Where's Leyanna?"

"She's downstairs with your son... Man, he's so adorable and fresh." She giggled, and I laughed when I thought of my baby boy.

I could have been taken from him, yet God had another plan me—for us. Benji left the room, and a few minutes later, he came back with my son in his arms.

"Baby," I said and looked at him getting crazy in his uncle's arms. He was trying to reach for me and started getting upset once he couldn't come into my arms. Benji sat him down right beside me and he climbed on me. I winced in pain, but I wasn't going to complain.

"Want me to move him, Mookie?"

"No, he's fine," I said as he laid his head right on my chest. My baby boy missed me, and I missed him. I closed my eyes when I heard his soft snores and held onto him. We both laid there, falling asleep in each other's arm. When I opened my eyes,

I caught the tail end of Benji leaving the room along with Aaliyah.

"You sleep?" Leyanna walked into the room.

I shook my head, and she came and gave me a gentle hug. "I was so worried about you, Chy. I'm so happy that you're up," she said and looked me over. "He missed his mama." She smiled and kissed my baby on the top of his head.

"I missed him too."

"Get some sleep, and I'll go get some food to cook some dinner. Benji won't move out of this house, so we've been staying here." She laughed.

I giggled because my big brother would forever be my protector. It didn't matter how old I was; Benji would forever be my first love and the person I knew would always have my back. Shutting my eyes, I laid back and took a nap with my son.

$$$

IT WAS PAINFUL, but I was up and walking. My lip didn't heal too much, but they planned to take the stitches out soon. Most of the days, I spent in this bedroom with the TV on and my son next to me. Tamar had come up with Myles to see me and check on her grandbaby. They took care of him most of the time while Leyanna was packing for the new house and running the boutique. Benji had been here the whole time until I told him to go and pack for his new home. Hesitantly, he did as I told him and went to help Leyanna.

"You good?" Kash walked into the room and leaned on the door. Since waking up, I hadn't seen Kash, and no one seemed to mention him.

Nodding my head, I climbed back into the bed. "I feel good, most days."

Most days, I felt good; then the others when I thought about what that nigga did to me, I would break down and cry. For the most part, I was handling it my way. Leyanna suggested I talk to a therapist about it. Aaliyah ended up going home to her mother's. She was going to stay there until she could get back into the dorms.

"I've been staying in a hotel to give y'all some room to deal with this." He walked further into the room.

"That's ridiculous; this is your home. Why not stay in a guest room?"

He shrugged his shoulders. "I feel guilty as fuck for this shit that happened to you, Princess."

Hearing him call me Princess brought up mixed emotions. "How could you have known this was going to happen? Don't blame yourself," I told him.

"But I do." He sighed and took a seat in the chair. "I love you and my son, and if I can't have y'all, I'm lost as fuck."

"Kash, you killed my mother. You killed my mother and then kept the secret from me. Too much has happened for us to move on like nothing ever happened. I aborted our baby, you killed my mother, and I'll never be able to trust you again."

"Understandable." He nodded, looking hurt.

I was hurt too, yet I couldn't do this relationship with him. It took a lot out of me to not tell Benji to kill him when he kept asking me. Baby Kash deserved a relationship with his father. If I killed him, it would be me doing the same exact thing I was hurt about him doing.

He touched my hand and put it in his. "You know you're my heart, and I love the shit out of you, Princess. I just wanna be able to raise my son with you."

"That's not a problem; we will always be friends, Kairo."

"Bet." He smiled, and we held hands as the room was silent. We both knew it was over for a relationship, yet I felt at peace about it. My mother felt at peace about it too.

EPILOGUE

LEYANNA

I GAVE birth to a ten-pound baby girl by the name of Carol Ellie Johnson. It was only right she was named after her grandmother that wasn't here in the flesh but here in spirit. Benji was there the whole time as he held my hand and we welcomed our daughter into the world. Now, I don't know if my body would ever go back to the same size because Benji was talking about trying for another one in a few months. That man was crazy if he thought I was having another one of his ten-pound big-headed babies. We moved into our home, and it was beautiful. Our daughter's nursery was ocean themed, and you could hear the waves right outside of her window. I honestly think that was why she slept through the night.

The store was doing amazing, and we were bringing in a good amount of money. Everybody wanted to visit the store and get some of the hottest clothes. Chyna decided that she wanted to be a part of the store again, and I welcomed her with opened arms. She was there more than me now, and she didn't leave the store closed for a week anymore. She didn't pick up school again because she claimed it wasn't for her. Benji was pissed, but I told him he had to let her run her own life. She wasn't his Mookie anymore; she was Chyna.

She moved into a condo right on Miami Beach with just she and Baby Kash, who was now walking and being a little terror. That little boy looked just like his father spit him out. Chyna and Kash weren't together, but they were co-parenting Baby Kash. Kash was in a new relationship with some chick named Veronica. She was nice, yet I couldn't be too nice because she was his new woman. Chyna didn't seem to be bothered by the fact that he had a new chick. I honestly thought it was because she was still sleeping with him.

Auntie Daisy had a baby boy and moved to upstate New York to be closer to her man in prison. Benji thought it was crazy, and I did too. Still, she came for holidays and called and checked on me and the baby. Benji ended up closing his sneaker store in New York and moving it to Miami since Daisy moved upstate. He was working out the kinks and was planning on opening it soon. I was enjoying having him home more often now.

JoJo and Renee welcomed another baby girl by the name Joel. She was the cutest thing ever and resembled her sister, Jolie. It was sad what happened to Lilly, and I was glad that JoJo and Renee stepped up and raised her along with her sister. They had just moved into a new house with space for Lilly's mother. JoJo took over the responsibility of caring for her. He said he knew that was what Lilly would have wanted. I commended him on stepping up and doing that. Jolie was happy to have a piece of her mother around too. As for Solace, the police had recovered video-tapes from the house. A new buyer bought the house and discovered a secret video room. They had the tape of him beating Lilly to death. He was now wanted for murder, but too bad he was dust.

Loving a hitta wasn't for everyone, and sometimes, things didn't end up working the way you wanted them to. I fell in love, got married, and now have a daughter with my husband—all the things I told him I didn't want to do. Chyna went from being engaged to single and working on herself. She had a lot of mental wounds she had to deal with, but she was doing just fine with it. With time, she would be able to be in a new and healthy relationship. I do believe Kash loved Chyna, and still loved her to this day. Chyna still loved Kash and wanted to be with him. You saw the love in both of their eyes; then, you could also see the hurt that they both were dealing with. It was comforting to know that whenever she needed him, he would drop anything to be there for her because the love was there. Sometimes, love wasn't always enough. Loving a hitta wasn't for everyone, but dammit, I sure did love mine.

THE END

COMING 10/09!

CPSIA information can be obtained
at www.ICGtesting.com
Printed in the USA
LVHW011616071218
599658LV00001B/129